R0061340659

12/2011

High Green Gun

High Green Gun

A SHAWN STARBUCK WESTERN

RAY HOGAN

SAGEBRUSH
Large Print Westerns

First published in Great Britain by ISIS Publishing Ltd
First published in the United States by Signet Books

Published in Large Print 2007 by ISIS Publishing Ltd.,
7 Centremead, Osney Mead, Oxford OX2 0ES
by arrangement with
Golden West Literary Agency

British Library Cataloguing in Publication Data
Hogan, Ray, 1908–
    High Green gun. – Large print ed. –
    (Sagebrush western series)
    1. Western stories
    2. Large type books
    I. Title
    813.5'2 [F]

ISBN 978–0–7531–7772–3 (hb)

Printed and bound in Great Britain by
T. J. International Ltd., Padstow, Cornwall

CHAPTER
ONE

Suddenly tense, Starbuck froze. He was crouched beside a small fire over which he was preparing his early-morning meal when a muffled sound caught his attention, and in that raw land where constant vigilance was the price of life, he had learned never to ignore the unperceived.

He had just set a can of water off the low flames, added the necessary amount of crushed coffee beans, and was in the process of stirring the combined bits of dried meat, potatoes, salt pork, and hard biscuits simmering in a spider into a thick porridge. It wasn't much of a meal, but he gave that little thought. He'd been near broke and out of trail grub before — and things had always changed for the better. Somewhere along the line he'd find work, accumulate a bit of cash with which to lay in a fresh stock of food, and then push on to continue the search for his brother, Ben.

Starvation was never a threat, anyway; there were always rabbits and birds to be snared, larger game to shoot, or fish to be taken from the streams, and he'd long ago become familiar with the edible plants that were to be found on the slopes and in the valleys. But a man could get mighty damned tired of his own fixings,

1

and signing on for a job meant not only money for his poke but sitting down to a table end enjoying regularly a stove-cooked meal prepared by someone else.

The winter hadn't been too bad for him, however, despite the fact his efforts to locate Ben had been fruitless. He'd spent the cold months drifting along the Mexican border making inquiries in the towns lying on both sides of the line, and come up with nothing. There were a lot of folks on the move, was the general gist of the replies he received; how could anybody be expected to remember one particular individual?

But Ben had passed that way; of that Starbuck was certain. He'd seen his brother late that previous year, a prisoner in the hands of a band of Comancheros high in the massive Sierra Madre range in Mexico. And then later he had enabled Ben and several other captives to escape from the Mexican outlaws — although none of them was aware of their benefactor's identity — and cross over into the safety of the United States.

He'd followed as quickly as it had been possible, since it appeared that the conclusion of those several years of search for his brother that he'd engaged in was at last about to be realized. But as in many previous instances — times that were slowly and surely dulling his determination to fulfill the obligation he had assumed upon the death of his father — he encountered another disappointment.

Nevertheless, he had resumed the quest, probing all the small settlements, the larger towns, the ranches and homesteads with a stubborn although growing cynicism, to no avail. Finally, when spring began to make itself known in the desert country by lifting the thorny fingers of the chollas and greening the thin grass that covered the flats and hillsides, he turned north. There'd be plenty of work to be found at that time of year on all the big cattle spreads, and as far as he could judge, his chances for finding Ben were about as good now one place as another.

A sardonic thought entered his mind as he hunkered near his fire halfway up the slope of the hills they called the Packsaddles; it could as easily be Ben Starbuck moving cautiously about out there in the brush as it could be some stranger, some outlaw running from a badge, a saddlebum headed for parts unknown even to him, or a cowhand doing his job. Only one thing was certain: it would not be an Indian. No brave would be so careless in his movements.

The noise came again — the quiet swishing of brush. It carried distinctly on the crisp mountain air, and was near enough this time to locate — somewhere off to his left. The sound was hesitant, indicating the person making it was approaching with care.

Starbuck rested the handle of the improvised spoon with which he was stirring his meal on the rim of the frying pan. Casually he drew himself upright, glanced to the sky in the east. The soft rustling had come from that direction. Turning, he moved to where he was facing the pale, predawn glare, now fading gradually as streaks of salmon and rose began to fuse the translucent pearl, and once more squatted by the fire.

The concoction in the skillet was ready to eat, but he took up the spoon, resumed the stirring. This time, however, his left hand was free, hung close to the forty-five Colt strapped to his thigh . . . He would be ready.

The moments dragged, the only sounds now being the busy burbling of the stew-like mixture in the spider and the distant cawing of crows rousing themselves for their flight from the slopes to feeding grounds somewhere below.

Starbuck swore impatiently under his breath. What the hell was the jasper holding back for? Was he going to make a move or continue skulking about in the brush? The faint scraping came again, the muted rasp of cloth raking against a branch of oak brush or some like growth; and then, once more, silence.

Whoever it was, now close by, was undoubtedly standing in the deep shadows observing him, Starbuck knew. He had the feeling of being watched, of having another man's eyes drilling into him — of perhaps being the object of a leveled gun.

Off to one side his sorrel stirred, shifted nervously. The big gelding, always a good sentinel, was aware of the intruder's presence also. Likely he had caught the smell of another horse.

Abruptly grim and entirely out of patience, Starbuck drew himself erect again. He'd be damned if he'd play another man's game! Moving deliberately, he turned toward the sorrel, picketed in the brush some half-dozen strides away, and crossed to where it was waiting. Reaching the horse, Starbuck began to examine the rope securing the animal as if to be certain the knot was holding.

4

Suddenly wheeling, he moved away from the big gelding, and ducking low, hurried along a narrow aisle of open ground between the pines and low-growing, tangled brush. Shortly his sweeping glance caught sight first of a bay horse standing off to his left, and then the figure of a man facing the camp.

Drawing his pistol, Starbuck closed in quickly. The interloper whirled at the sound of his approach. His eyes spread and his hands went over his head in a frantic gesture of no resistance.

"Wait . . ."

"Keep your arms up!" Starbuck snapped.

Looking about to make certain the man was alone, and seeing no sign of anyone else, Starbuck stepped in close. Lifting the weapon from the holster on the intruder's hip, he shoved it under his own belt and motioned toward the fire, visible through the screen of leaves and branches some twenty feet or so away.

"Move!" Starbuck ordered coldly, pushing the man toward the camp. "You've been spying on me. Now I aim to have a look at you."

CHAPTER
TWO

The bay standing back in the brush stirred anxiously, as if he thought he was being deserted.

"My horse — I ought to . . ."

"Forget it. Can see to him later."

They reached the small clearing, and the intruder, hands still above his head, halted by the fire. He glanced down at the simmering contents of the skillet, swallowed hard. Unmoved, Starbuck studied him narrowly.

He was a lean, whiplike man, probably in his mid-twenties. His hair was dark and his eyes were small in a somewhat narrow face that bore a pinched look. His clothing — checked shirt, black-leather vest, cord pants tucked into scarred, stovepipe boots, dusty, flat-crowned hat — all appeared to be a bit large for him. A full cartridge belt encircled his waist, and the holster on his hip, dark from much oiling, had been cut low to make the well-worn weapon it contained more readily accessible.

"Who the hell are you, and what do you want?" Starbuck demanded, still angry.

"Name's Boone Trevison. Smelled your cooking, aimed to ask if you could spare a bite of whatever's in that frying pan, along with a cup of java."

Starbuck swore feelingly. "Way you went about doing it could've got you killed!" he snapped. "Why didn't you sing out like a man usually does instead of skulking around there in the bushes?"

"Was intending to — just had to make sure I wasn't walking into trouble," Trevison replied.

Back up on the slope of the mountain a grouse drummed noisily as Starbuck continued to study the man. Finally he shrugged, put away his weapon.

"Cup and plate there in my grub sack," he said, motioning toward his saddle, placed across a nearby log. "Help yourself."

Trevison, a tight grin on his thin lips, nodded, complied at once. Starbuck, arms folded across his chest, waited until the man had taken his portions, and then, filling his own utensils, moved to the opposite side of the fire where he could face his unexpected visitor, and squatting down, shoulders against the trunk of a pine, began to eat. Boone Trevison seemed to be nothing more or less than he claimed — a hungry man needing a meal — but Starbuck, never one to take anything for granted, did not lower his guard.

For one thing, what was Trevison doing on the trail without a supply of grub? Of course, he could have in some way lost his stock, but that seemed unlikely, just as did the possibility of his having simply run out. Certainly no man would have started off across country before provisioning himself; towns and ranches were too few and far between to depend on them as a source, and Trevison, judging from his gear, was no greenhorn.

"Which way you headed?" Starbuck asked, finishing off his plate and turning to his coffee.

Trevison, his portion of food also gone, glanced questioningly at the bit remaining in the spider.

"Go ahead, clean it up," Starbuck said.

Trevison's hunger had been deep, there was no doubt of that, but such still did not excuse the manner in which he had approached the camp. Most men in Starbuck's position would have opened fire first and asked questions later. Features expressionless, he watched the tall man dump the last of the stew into his plate and go after it eagerly. His coffee was yet untouched.

"Which way are you riding?" Starbuck asked, repeating himself.

"Looking for a place called High Green," Boone replied between mouthfuls. "Ranch around here somewheres."

High Green . . . It struck no familiar note in Shawn Starbuck's mind. But that meant nothing; he was in that particular area of the territory for the first time himself.

"You ever hear of it?"

Starbuck shook his head. "This is big country. Man needs better directions than just saying it's around here somewhere. Expect it'll be a place back up in the high country, going by that name."

"Got a job waiting for me there. Somehow lost myself trying to find it."

"Punching cows?"

"Not for sure what," Trevison said, setting his well-cleaned plate aside. Reaching into a shirt pocket, he produced an envelope. "Letter here tells me to come," he added, and leaning forward, tossed it to Starbuck.

Shawn caught the creased oblong of thumbed paper, and relinquishing his cup, unfolded it and glanced at the address. It was made out to Boone Trevison, General Delivery, Fort Worth, Texas. Removing the sheet of paper it contained, he scanned the writing.

It stated sparingly there was a job open on the ranch, that a Denver cattle buyer named John Yocum had referred the writer to him, declaring him to be a reliable and able man. If he was looking for work he was to report as soon as possible. Also, if he wished to bring any friends he was willing to vouch for, to do so. The letter was signed Aaron Kraft, owner of High Green Ranch.

"Written by a woman," Starbuck commented, returning the paper to its envelope and passing it back to Boone. "How long since you got it?"

Trevison brushed at his thin moustache. "Couple of weeks. Was waiting for me at the post office. Don't know how long it'd been there. Couldn't read the date. Been smeared."

"Noticed that. Chance you're too late. Spring cow work's already started at most ranches around here."

"Could be," Trevison admitted. "Gamble I'll be taking, anyway. You just riding through, or are you looking for work?"

"Can use a job, all right," Shawn said. "Was heading up Montana way, though. Always plenty of work to be found around there this time of the year."

Trevison drained his cup, produced a sack of tobacco and a fold of cigarette papers. "Smoke?"

Starbuck waved off the offer. "Habit I don't have yet," he said, and fell silent as Boone twisted himself a thin cylinder of tobacco.

There was no good reason why he shouldn't take Trevison's suggestion. The letter from rancher Kraft had invited the rider to bring along any friends wanting a job, and it would spare him a long trip north.

"Where you been working?" Boone asked, scraping a match into fire against a handy rock.

"No place special for the last few months. Been down along the border looking for my brother."

Trevison lit his cigarette, inhaled deeply, expelled a cloud of thin blue smoke. On a rotting log beyond him a small chipmunk had abruptly appeared, its eyes bright and curious, the stripes on its face looking like painted-on bars of black and white.

"Your brother? He lost or something?"

"In a way," Shawn said with a dry smile. "Left home — back in Ohio — when he wasn't much more than a kid. Need to find him so's the family estate can be settled."

"I see," Trevison murmured. Then, "Like you said, this is big country. Expect locating him'll be quite a chore."

10

"Got close down in Mexico a time back — closest I've ever been, in fact — and then lost him again. You come here from Texas?"

"Yeh. Was down around New Orleans for a spell, but Texas is my home."

"Fort Worth?"

"Yeh, was born right close by," Trevison said.

"Chance Ben, my brother, was around there. Always ask every man I run into if he's seen him. Could be you have."

Boone nodded. "Could be — I never got your name."

"Starbuck — Shawn Starbuck. Brother's name is Ben, but he goes by Damon Friend, mostly."

Trevison gave that thought, shrugged after a bit. "Sure don't sound familiar . . . Why two names? He having trouble with the law?"

"No, was so worked up when he ran off after the squabble with my pa that he quit the family name."

"I see," Trevison said. The sun was now out, and light was filling the glade. "He look like you?"

"Pretty strong resemblance. Ben's a mite older and heavier. Don't think anybody'd have trouble telling that we're related."

Boone's cigarette had gone cold. Leaning forward, he plucked a burning twig from the fire, held it to the short stub. At his movement the chipmunk bolted from the log and disappeared into the ground litter.

"I think I would've remembered him if I'd ever run across him. How long've you been looking?"

"Going on five years now," Starbuck said a bit wearily.

The heaviness in his voice was not lost on Trevison. "Can see you're getting a bit tired of it."

Shawn smiled wryly. "There're a few things I'd like to do with my life — specially if I can get my share of Pa's estate. Way it's going, I'll never get the chance."

"You tried leaving word for him, maybe even posting a reward with the law in some of the bigger towns around the country?"

"Done that — leastwise, I've left word plenty of places, and I'm pretty sure he knows I'm trying to get in touch with him. Get the idea now and then he's dodging me."

"Why'd he do that?"

"Probably figures Pa sent me to bring him back. He wouldn't know that Pa's dead . . . And that reward idea you mentioned, I've thought of it. Even talked it over with a couple of lawmen I got acquainted with, and it could be the answer, only some bounty hunter might get it in his head that Ben was an outlaw and use a gun to bring him in. Seeing a notice posted in some marshal's office could make them think so."

"Never thought about it that way," Trevison said, flipping the dead cigarette but into the smoldering fire. Rising, he smiled, nodded. "Sure obliged to you for the meal. Run out of grub myself a couple of days back."

Starbuck got to his feet. "You're welcome, of course," he said, and taking the worn forty-five from his waistband, handed it to Trevison. "You'll be wanting this."

12

Boone took the weapon, and scarcely glancing at it, dropped it into its holster.

"You been thinking any about hiring on at High Green with me? Be proud to have your company."

"Job's a job," Starbuck said. "Doesn't make much difference to me whose range I'm riding, long as I draw wages for doing it."

Trevison grinned broadly, clearly pleased at Shawn's decision. "Reckon that leaves us with only one problem — finding the place."

Starbuck half-turned, pointed to a smoke haze hanging in the sky to the north. "Looks like a town on up the flat a ways. Can go there, ask some questions."

"Ain't too far, either," Trevison said, nodding, and began to gather the utensils used for the meal. "Reckon we'll have to leave these go without washing, unless you got water in your canteen. Mine's dry."

Starbuck glanced about, pointed to a close-by arroyo. "I'll scrub them out with sand. Better bring up your horse. Can take what I've got left for him and my sorrel. Use the skillet so's you won't waste any. Likely a stream on ahead somewheres, but we'd best not figure on it . . . I'll be getting my gear together while you're doing it."

Shawn moved off toward the narrow wash, taking the plates and spoons, leaving the spider for Trevison's use. He heard the man move on by in the direction of his bay horse, saw him return in only moments with the animal, a strong-looking gelding with a Circle A brand on its left hip. The saddle was well used, and there was no rifle in the boot hanging from it. Evidently Boone

Trevison slept cold, as no blanket roll was tied behind the cantle of the old hull.

By the time the tall rider had completed the task of watering the two horses, Starbuck had put his gear back together and was saddling the sorrel. As he finished up, Trevison mounted his bay and sat idly waiting, watching Shawn's movements.

"Can tell you and that horse've been together a long time," he commented when Starbuck, finally ready, swung onto the gelding. "He seems to know just what you're doing and when you're going to do it."

Shawn smiled. "We have," he said, and led the way out of the small clearing for the flat below.

CHAPTER
THREE

The flat, walled by a high range of mountains to the west and running on indefinitely to the east, was floored with grama and tufted timothy. Trees, mostly cottonwoods, clustered about water holes here and there, and the blur of a ranchhouse with its accompanying structures appeared occasionally in the distance. It was a rich land, that was evident, and a man should do well with cattle or anything else he set his hand to raising.

It would be a fine place for horses, Starbuck thought, the old, often-entertained dream of owning such a ranch once again making itself known. With his share of Hiram Starbuck's estate, somewhere in the neighborhood of fifteen thousand dollars, he could go far in buying fine breeding stock and providing the proper and necessary equipment and facilities for raising and training good horses.

Admittedly, the price of the average mount was low, but there was always a market for better stock and a willingness on the part of buyers to pay more for top-grade horseflesh — animals that combined the outstanding qualities of size, intelligence, strength, staying power, and that had not been broken in spirit while being accustomed to the saddle.

It was a recurring dream of Starbuck's, one in which he had indulged often, but always it faded off into the harsh background of reality when he faced the knowledge that he could not hope to settle down until he had fulfilled his obligation — that of finding Ben and satisfying his father's wishes.

Shrugging, he glanced at the man riding an arm's length to his left. Did he, too, have hopes, dreams, the wish to build for himself a way of life that appealed to him? He, too, was a drifter — it showed plainly — but was it by choice or for some reason? At the moment Boone's features were stilled, his gaze fixed on the pall of smoke marking the location of whatever town it was that now lay just beyond a rise not far ahead. If he was struck by the beauty of the lush country around him, it did not manifest itself.

And then, as if aware of the attention being accorded him, Trevison turned to Starbuck. "Was wondering about that belt buckle you're wearing. You one of them fancy boxers, or it just something you picked up?"

Shawn reached down, let his fingers travel over the oblong of ornately scrolled silver with its ivory figure of a fighter posed in traditional stance.

"Was my pa's. He used to put on exhibition matches back home — not for money, just because he liked to. Got his training from some Englishman."

"He ever a champion?"

16

"No. Didn't want to be, but I expect he could have if ever he'd taken the notion. I saw him box some mighty good men, and far as I know, he never was beaten."

"Buckle came to you when he died, that it?"

Shawn nodded.

"How about the boxing part? He teach you how to use your fists the way he did?"

"Taught both my brother and me. Ben puts on a match now and then to earn cash, I've found out, so I guess he's about as good as Pa."

"What about you?"

"Fight when I have to. Not interested in doing it as a way to make a living."

Trevison lapsed into silence as the horses continued their easy lope toward the crown of the rise. Far back on the mountain slopes to the west a lone gunshot echoed faintly. Both men turned, glanced briefly in the direction of the sound, and then resumed their positions. Shortly they topped out on the crest, slowed as the road forked, one branch cutting due east, the other continuing on north for the scatter of buildings and accompanying houses lying in a shallow at the foot of the mountain.

"Carsonville," Trevison said, reading a faded sign pointing toward the settlement. "Reckon that's where we're headed."

Starbuck's attention was on the towering hills to the west. Aaron Kraft's High Green spread would be somewhere on their slopes, he supposed, likely in one of the broad valleys; they would know for certain when they reached the town and made inquiries. If no one knew of Kraft, then Trevison had come to the wrong part of the territory — and he'd as well forget about it and go on to Montana.

"Pretty fair-looking burg," he heard Boone say, and lifting his glance, Starbuck let his eyes take in the settlement as they swung onto the street.

Whistler's General Store, Bell's Livery Stable, the Emporium, Ladies' & Gents' Furnishings, the Cattleking saloon — the name spelled as if it was one word . . . The Breckenridge House, Moriarty's Restaurant, the Longhorn saloon. The widely spreading steer horns affixed to the front of that establishment as a bit of material designation showed considerable bullet damage attesting to the occasional high spirits of its customers.

Starbuck's idle glance ran on, assessing the town, judging it by the hundred or more others he'd ridden into at previous times and under similar circumstances . . . Will Lovan, Blacksmith & Iron Molder, Bolton's Feed & Seed Store, Austin's Gun & Saddle Shop, the Packsaddle Flats Bank . . . a row of small offices including that of J. Eiseman, M.D., an attorney, Will Norman, a hall bearing the emblem of the Masonic and Odd Fellows lodges, apparently used jointly but not concurrently. There were two churches, one with a steeple, the other with a square belfry . . . The jail — this one with a neatly lettered nameplate bearing the inscription "John Coon, Town Marshal."

Carsonville was a well-ordered, prosperous-appearing town, which spoke well for the ranchers and other landowners on the far-reaching flat east of the mountains, and the lonely hope of having his own holdings once again stirred within Starbuck.

"Where'll we go to do our asking?" Trevison wondered, breaking into Shawn's thoughts.

Starbuck stared at the man briefly as if surprised at the question, then jerked a thumb at the Cattleking. "Biggest saloon's always the best bet."

Boone nodded, frowned, considered the dozen or so persons moving along the board sidewalks. "Might save time to just pull up, ask somebody passing by — or go to the marshal's office. It's right there, ahead."

Starbuck again studied Trevison thoughtfully, shrugged. Boone apparently hadn't done much traveling about, or he wouldn't suggest going to a lawman for such information. While he had nothing against men who wore a star, he knew them ordinarily to be instantly and automatically suspicious of strangers riding into their town, and only too often a simple, harmless question put to them led to delay and problems. Such was a well-established fact along the trails, and he was surprised that Boone was unaware of or chose to ignore it.

"Let's stick with the saloon. Bartenders always know everybody in the country. Could use a drink, anyway."

Trevison made no reply, and they continued on until they were in front of the Cattleking's high wooden facade, and there curved into its hitchrack. Three horses were at the long post, and Shawn reckoned business was slow, which was what could be expected at that hour of the day.

Dismounting, they wrapped their leathers about the crossbar, climbed the single step to the narrow porch extending out from the building, and pushed through the batwing doors into the shadowy, redolent saloon.

The bar stood against the opposite wall, and the riders of the horses waiting in the street were lined up before it. Elsewhere in the dimly lit building a swamper was moving slowly about among the chairs and tables performing his cleaning duties.

"Rye whiskey," Starbuck said as he and Trevison took places at the counter and faced the solitary barkeep, who broke off conversation with his three customers and edged toward them.

"Same for me," Boone said.

The man bucked his head crisply, reached for glasses and a bottle. He wore no apron, worked only in vest, pants, and shirt open at the neck. Most likely he was the owner of the Cattleking, on duty during the slack period preceding the busy evenings, when regulars took over the chore.

"Be four bits," the round-faced man stated as he filled the thick-bottomed shot glasses.

Starbuck laid a silver dollar on the counter without waiting for Trevison to reach into his pocket, and taking up the drink, downed it in a single gulp. It was good whiskey.

"Once more," he said as the bartender shoved change toward him. Turning to Trevison, he lifted his brows questioningly. "Another'n for you?"

Boone, glass half-empty, finished it off and nodded. The man behind the counter reclaimed the two quarters, poured the refills, and started to turn away.

"Kraft's place — High Green, I think it's called," Starbuck said. "You tell us how to get there?"

The barkeep paused, cast a side glance at the trio of hard-looking cowhands farther down the counter. Shawn followed his lead with a shifting of his own attention. The riders had swung their gaze to him and Trevison, and one, a broad-faced redhead with a ragged growth of beard, was setting his drink back onto the bar. Starbuck's eyes narrowed. He came back to the bartender.

"Well?"

The man swallowed, nodded. "Kraft's? Yeh, he's got a place about ten miles west of here."

"He call it High Green?"

"That's what he does —"

"We're hiring out to him," Boone cut in, smiling. "Any special way of getting there?"

"Not that I know of. Just keep riding on through town till you come to a fork in the road. Take the left hand, the one west toward the mountain. It'll lead you to Kraft's place."

Starbuck, tossing off his second drink, came about slowly. The three hardcases had pulled away from the counter, were moving up. The redhead, swaggering, had pushed his hat to the back of his head. There was a smirk on his coarse features.

"I hear you telling you was going to work for Kraft?" he asked, halting in front of Shawn.

Starbuck looked the man over coldly. The pair siding him had taken up a stand at either shoulder and a step behind.

"Now, Charlie — hold on," the bartender began in an anxious voice.

"Keep out of this!" the redhead snapped, hooking his thumbs in his gunbelt. Advancing another half-stride, he stared at Starbuck. "Asked you a question, mister!"

"I heard you," Shawn replied, temper lifting. "Can't see that it's any of your damned business, but the answer's yes."

Charlie's head came forward belligerently. "Making it my business," he said. "And I'm telling you this one time — keep on riding. Ain't you or nobody else going to work for High Green!"

CHAPTER
FOUR

"You're wasting your breath," Starbuck said coolly, and beckoning to Trevison, added, "Let's go."

"Not till I'm done talking!" Charlie shouted, and lunged.

Shawn, keyed to the moment, pivoted, sidestepped. As the redhead lurched toward him, he caught the rider by one shoulder. Whirling him around, he shoved him back into the arms of his two companions.

"Better look after him," he said in a grim, promising way, and continued on for the doorway.

"Look out!"

The warning came from Boone Trevison. Starbuck spun. Charlie's hand was sweeping down, reaching for the pistol on his hip. Anger swept through Shawn as an oath escaped his tight lips. He lashed out with a foot. The toe of his boot struck the redhead's gun as it was clearing leather, sent it skittering across the saloon's floor.

Jaw set, Starbuck closed in on Charlie. Fists cocked, he jabbed a left into the man's face, crossed with a right to the jaw. Charlie staggered, caught himself. Legs spread, head thrust forward, arms hanging at his sides, he glared at Shawn.

"That there's going to cost you aplenty," he growled, and again threw himself at Starbuck.

Shawn again sidestepped the headlong charge. Cool, he hooked a fist into Charlie's belly, landed a sharp right to the head — and staggered as a blow to the neck from somewhere behind him all but drove him to his knees. A fresh wave of anger rocked him. He pivoted unsteadily, came face-to-face with one of Charlie's friends — the husky blond. Off to the left he saw the other — the tall, gamblerlike rider — circling to get at him from the opposite side.

A fist to the jaw rocked Starbuck solidly. Charlie . . . The redhead was moving in on him from the front. Shawn wheeled away from the three men, dropped subconsciously into a fighting stance . . . Where the hell was Trevison?

"Well, looky there!" the redhead shouted gleefully. "He's one of them dancer jaybirds! Come on, let's get him. Bill, you take the left side, Al, you nail him from the right. I'll handle the front. Reckon we ought to show him how real fighting's done around here."

Bill — that was the thick-shouldered blond. Shawn jabbed with a left as the rider stepped toward him, completed with a right that spun the squat man half about and stalled him. Starbuck, foremost in his mind old Hiram's admonition never to let anger get the best of him in a fight and thereby leave himself open for mistakes, pulled away. Bending slightly, he backhanded Al across the face, surged into Charlie. Hammering two rapid blows into the man's middle, he came up with

24

both fists, rapped the redhead sharply on the nose, bringing a quick spurt of blood.

As Charlie howled a curse, Shawn endeavored to cut away, gasped as Bill drove rock-hard knuckles into his side, sent a jab of pain through him. He reeled, struck out at a shadowy figure crowding in on him from the opposite side — unaware of just which of the three men it was.

He was beginning to suck hard for wind, and sweat was now covering his face and misting his eyes. Falling back a few steps, he lashed out at Charlie, coming straight at him. The stinging blow to the face slowed the redhead, wiped the grin from his lips. Shawn flung a glance toward the bar. Boone Trevison was standing motionless, transfixed, either unwilling or unable to act.

"Damnit — give me a hand!" Starbuck rasped. "Get one of them off my back."

He staggered as both Bill and Charlie rushed into him, fists flailing. He dodged the wild blows as best he could for a few seconds, endeavoring to take them where they would do the least damage, and then suddenly raging, he surged forward, smashed the husky blond solidly on the chin as the opening presented itself.

Bill sagged to his knees, hands down, arms limp, and Starbuck, moving like a shadow, feinted, spun, closed in on Charlie. He drove a whistling left and a right to the man's face, wheeled away, now searching for Al. He muttered in satisfaction. The tall, dark man was standing off to his left, hands over his head. Trevison, pistol drawn, had taken him out of the fight.

A half-dozen men were now lined up along the counter looking on. Apparently they had heard the sounds of scuffling as they were passing the doorway of the Cattleking, had entered to see what was taking place. All were watching silently, and since there was no cheering and they were voicing no encouragement, he reckoned they were not friends of Charlie's and the pair backing him. The swamper had ceased his activities, was also looking on from behind the counter, where he was standing beside the bartender.

Motion on the floor to one side brought Shawn's attention around. Bill was slowly, unsteadily pulling himself upright, had reached the point where he was on hands and knees. Starbuck raised a foot, placed it against the shoulder of the squat rider, sent him sprawling back onto the floor. He wheeled then to Charlie.

"Just us now," he said in a low, savage voice, and moved in on the redhead.

Charlie, face covered with sweat and smeared with blood, threw a hasty glance to Al, another to the recumbent, motionless figure of Bill, and took a quick step backward. Starbuck struck out with a wide, swinging right. It landed on the man's shoulder, rocked him off balance, stalled him.

"Odds all wrong for you now, Red?" he taunted, brushing at the moisture clouding his eyes.

Charlie swore, lunged, arms outstretched and fingers clawing. Shawn allowed him to draw near, suddenly reached out, boxed the man's ears soundly with open palms. The redhead yelled with pain, halted. Starbuck ripped a straight left to the belly, followed with a right that thudded solidly as it connected with the rider's jaw.

Charlie reeled, retreated unsteadily. Starbuck, heaving for breath, eyes burning and remorseless as those of a big mountain cat moving in for the kill, continued the attack. Jabbing the redhead sharply in the face, he sent another smashing blow to his jaw. Charlie's knees began to buckle. Shawn caught him by the shirt front, and supporting him with one hand, drove his fist again into the man's jaw.

The redhead groaned, began to sink. Shawn's arm drew back for a third punishing blow. He hesitated. Charlie's eyes were rolling helplessly. Abruptly Starbuck released his grip on the rider, allowed him to fall.

Pivoting, face shining with sweat, breath now coming in quick blasts, Shawn confronted Al. The tall man, arms still raised under the threat of Boone Trevison's pistol, fell back slightly before Starbuck's blazing glare.

"Your turn now," Shawn grated.

Al frowned, shook his head. "Ain't much of a fighter with my fists . . ."

"Makes no difference to me how we go — fists or guns," Starbuck snarled. "You name it, I'll accommodate you."

Al glanced about to the men standing at the bar and then to his friends sprawled on the floor. Again he wagged his head.

"This here's Charlie Vine's fight more'n it is mine. Was him that started it. Reckon I'd best let him finish it."

"Didn't notice you holding back any . . ."

Al's shoulders twitched. "Us that works for Ford Lalicker sticks together."

Starbuck, cooling slowly, settled back on his heels. "Who the hell's Lalicker?"

"Reckon you'll find out soon enough if you hang around Kraft's," Al replied.

Shawn sighed quietly. Lalicker apparently was another rancher in the Packsaddle country, and evidently no friend of Aaron Kraft's, judging from the attitude displayed by the redhead, Charlie Vine, and the pair with him. Just what was he letting himself in for at High Green?

Breathing normally now, Starbuck sleeved the sweat from his face, and stepping to one side, retrieved his hat from the floor, and drew it on.

"Put it away, Boone," he said, nodding at the pistol in Trevison's hand. "I guess our friend there's done all he aims to."

Trevison grinned, holstered his weapon. The men at the counter relaxed their tense positions, one beckoning to the bartender for service.

"Don't you be figuring this is over," Al said, finding a measure of courage. "Charlie sure ain't going to forget this."

Shawn nodded. "What I'd expect . . . Well, when he wakes up, you tell him he can find us at Kraft's anytime he takes the notion."

Wheeling, Starbuck, with Trevison at his side, moved for the doorway.

CHAPTER
FIVE

Two more men were standing just outside the Cattleking's batwings on the porch as Starbuck and Trevison left the saloon. They drew back, regarding Shawn in a curious but respectful silence as he crossed the wooden floor, stepped down into the dust, and rigidly made his way to the hitchrack.

Sweeping the walks with a still-sulfurous glance, he freed the sorrel's leathers and swung onto the saddle. Nearby Boone climbed aboard his bay, and then together they wheeled about and headed off down the street.

"That was one hell of a scrap," Boone murmured admiringly. "Got to say you —"

"Could've used some help from you," Starbuck replied stiffly. Reaching up, he probed the side of his jaw tenderly where Charlie Vine or one of the other men had succeeded in tagging him solidly.

"Didn't figure you was needing any help — or wanted it," Trevison said. "Anyway, I'd've just been underfoot. Never was much with my fists."

Shawn considered that quietly. He had come up against few men during the years he'd roamed the frontier who could not give a pretty fair accounting of themselves in a fight. It was more or less a necessity, but of course there were the exceptions — chiefly the men whose skill lay in their expertise with a pistol.

Such individuals ordinarily avoided any possible injury to their hands that could be sustained in a brawl — broken fingers, stiff knuckles, and the like, any of which could seriously affect their speed and dexterity with a gun.

Was that Boone Trevison's reason for standing back, and when he did finally cut himself in, doing so with the aid of his gun? Starbuck studied his companion covertly. The weapon he carried was worn, well used. Trevison himself, however, had the look of an ordinary cowhand, but it never paid to judge from appearances; Clay Allison, that peerless killer of the Cimarron with whom he'd by chance become acquainted when he first began the search for Ben, was a friendly, soft-spoken man with an engaging smile who could have easily been taken for a storekeeper.

"Reckon this here's where we turn off," he heard Boone say, and shifting his attention to the split in the road that lay just beyond the edge of town, followed the man onto the left branch that ran arrow-straight for the mountains to the west.

"What do you figure that whoop-tee-do there in the saloon was all about?" Trevison wondered as the horses settled into an easy lope. "Why'd them three be so dead-set on us not going to work for this man Kraft?"

Starbuck twisted slightly on the saddle, seeking relief from a dull aching in his side. "Some sort of trouble going on around here — between Kraft and the fellow they're working for. I think one of them called him Lalicker."

"Range war?" Boone said, his tone rising.

"Could be," Shawn answered, and again considered the man beside him. "That make a difference to you?"

Trevison hawked, spat. "Nope, sure don't. Job's a job, far as I'm concerned."

Starbuck turned back to the well-traveled road, lifting steadily to meet the green hills ahead. For his money he hoped they weren't riding into a range war; he'd been that route before, and he'd as soon not get himself involved again. Night riders, bushwhackers, fires, ambushes, always having to be on the alert — it was not a way of life he enjoyed, and if that was what it turned out to be once they met with Aaron Kraft and talked the situation over, he just might back off and ride on. He'd seen enough killing in Mexico.

But it would be a fine country to work out the summer and fall in, he thought, glancing about. They had reached the first of the trees, tall, ponderosa pines, squat piñons and cedars, oaks, an occasional locust and red-berried ash. The Packsaddles were high country but still somewhat below the line where the aspens and other rarefied-altitude trees were common.

The open meadows were thick with fescue and timothy, and shrubs — thimbleberry, currant, bitterbrush, oak, and the like — studded the slopes. Iris, their diamond-shaped blue buds near to the point of unfurling, columbine, yarrow, asters, and a host of other flowers yet to show their blossoms lay in close communities here and there.

31

"Man's mighty lucky to have himself a ranch in country like this," Boone observed. "Can easy understand why he'd fight to hold it."

Or others would try to take it from him, Shawn thought, eyes on a herd of cattle grazing in a broad swale to their right. They had topped out the first rise, were dropping gently into a wide valley. A sparkle of water coming down from the higher regions and slicing diagonally across the vast meadow caught his attention . . . If this was High Green range, it was choice property for certain.

Shifting on his saddle, he stared back over the road they were following. A big man, topping six feet and weighing a lean, muscular hundred and eighty pounds, he sat his horse with the grace of a natural rider. Dark hair worn long on his neck, a full moustache, deep-set blue-gray eyes squinting now to cut out some of the sun's glare, he looked to be just what he was — a hardened, experienced rider of the numberless trails that crisscrossed the limitless West.

There was at once to him a sort of coolness, a kind of reserve that neither took nor gave, but simply established him as a man on his own, one fully competent in all things that pertained to him. South of the border, where he had earned the respect of the Mexican people, he had been termed by them a *macho*, but if the complimentary appellation, the loose translation in English of which was "one hell of a man," aroused any particular pride within him, it never came to the surface.

"Ought to be getting there, seems."

Trevison's comment brought Starbuck back around. Ten miles, the bartender in the Cattleking had said. They had covered about that distance.

"Ought to be," Shawn agreed, and pointed toward the north. "Smoke there above those bluffs. Expect that's where the ranchhouse is."

Boone shaded his eyes, looked off into the distance at the faint haze hanging in the cloudless sky.

"Going to be a good ten miles," he muttered.

The land around them was becoming increasingly rougher, and Starbuck saw they were passing over a second rise, this one more of a rocky hogback than the first. The larger trees had thinned out, giving way to brush clumps and growth able to find purchase in the hard, gravelly soil. But it would be of short duration; he could see the green meadows and tall trees closing in again on the trail only a short distance beyond the crest of the rise.

"You reckon this here's such a smart idea, going to work for Kraft?" Trevison asked suddenly.

"Maybe, maybe not," Starbuck said indifferently. "Need to know what it's all about."

"I'm getting a bad feeling about things — like we was maybe biting off more'n we could chew."

"Trouble of some kind around here, that's for sure. Didn't figure that'd bother you any, however."

"Not saying it would," Trevison said hastily. "But I just keep wondering what we're walking into."

"Won't hurt to find out. Can always back off if we don't like the smell of things. I'm not anxious to mix myself up in a range war."

"You reckon that's what it is?"

Starbuck shrugged, waited as the horses, their ironshod hooves clattering noisily on hard rock, topped out the hogback and started down the opposite side.

Then: "It's got all the earmarks."

"You been through one before?"

"Couple of times," Shawn said. "As soon not sign up for another — not that I'm scared of dying. That'll happen someday, no matter what, but I —"

"Be far enough, gents!"

At the sharp command coming from the tall brush along the shoulder of the trail, Starbuck reined in quickly. He heard Boone Trevison swear in surprise as he drew to a halt. Hand already on the butt of his pistol, Starbuck let it go, shifted impatiently on his saddle as several riders, guns leveled, moved into view from both sides. Going to work for Aaron Kraft was turning out to be a big chore.

CHAPTER
SIX

"This here's High Green range," the rider in the center of the party said coldly. He was an elderly man, wore a new red bandanna about his neck that still showed the creases where it had been folded. "It's closed, and you ain't got no business crossing it . . . You going to say you didn't know that?"

"I'm going to say we're sort've getting the idea," Starbuck replied humorlessly.

The older man bristled. "Now, what the hell's that supposed to mean?"

"My partner here's got a letter from your boss, if his name's Kraft, inviting us to drop by," Shawn said, and nodded at Trevison.

Boone's hand darted abruptly toward a pocket. Instantly the riders stiffened, came to wary attention. Starbuck shook his head.

"Ease off. He's only getting the letter," he said patiently.

What the hell was Trevison thinking of? A sudden move like that could have gotten them both killed. Either he was careless or didn't give a damn.

Boone, holding the envelope, removed the sheet of paper from it and passed it to Kraft's man. "I'm

Trevison, the one it's addressed to. My friend here's Shawn Starbuck."

The old rider was staring at Boone, the letter still unread. "You're Trevison?"

Boone nodded. "I'm a mite late getting here, but that envelope laid in the post office for a spell, I expect, before I got it."

The older man glanced at the paper, handed it back. "It's all right, boys," he said over his shoulder to the men backing him. "Go on about your work. Be catching up shortly."

The riders swung away, rode off toward the south. The elderly cowhand watched them briefly, and then, spurring up nearer, extended his hand.

"I'm Hugh Dixon. Me and them fellows was moving some stock down to the east meadows when we seen you coming up the slope. Was Mr. Kraft's orders that we was to stop anybody passing through that ain't High Green. I'm real sorry about you two, but we didn't have no way of knowing."

"No harm done," Trevison said, returning the letter to its place. "You seem to be having trouble of some kind."

"That's sure the truth!" Dixon said wryly, turning to Shawn and offering his hand to him also. "I'm powerful glad you've showed up." He paused, frowned, studied the dark bruise on Starbuck's face. "You get yourself in some kind of fracas coming here?"

"In town," Trevison said before Shawn could make any reply. "Three men jumped us in the saloon. My friend took care of them."

36

"Three of them," Dixon repeated thoughtfully. "They wouldn't be going by the name of Charlie Vine and Bill Bristol and Al Rearick, would they?"

"That's what they answered to," Boone said. "Said something about some jasper called Lalicker, too."

Dixon bobbed. "Fellow they work for — Ford Lalicker. Supposed to be regular cowhands. Truth is, they're hired gunnies, and . . ."

The old rider broke off, swallowed hard. "I ain't meaning nothing by that. Was only —"

"Forget it," Starbuck said. A job with Aaron Kraft was looking less and less attractive. He leaned forward, rested a forearm on the horn of his saddle. "What's this Ford Lalicker want with gunslingers?"

"Same thing Mr. Kraft does — needs some strong backing."

"There a range war going on around here?" Boone asked.

"Well, maybe it ain't exactly that yet — and maybe it is," Dixon said. "Best you do your talking to Mr. Kraft about it."

"Expect we'd better. Where'll we find him?"

"Could be at the house this time of day. Just keep following the road," Dixon said, wheeling about. "Be seeing you later, I reckon."

Starbuck, his face expressionless, remained motionless, eyes on Hugh Dixon as the man hurried to overtake the other High Green riders. The old cowhand clearly didn't want to discuss the trouble Kraft was having with Ford Lalicker, but it called for hired guns on both sides, and that had the sound of a full-blown range war. He felt the press of Trevison's steady gaze, turned to him.

"You backing off?" Boone asked.

Shawn brushed his hat to the back of his head, wiped at the sweat on his face, wincing a bit when his fingers pressed the dark area of the bruise.

"Thinking about it . . . Don't remember you saying you were hiring your gun out to Kraft. Somehow got the idea it was a cowpunching job."

Trevison stirred. "No, guess I didn't talk too much about it."

"Dixon sounded like that was the deal from the start — that they'd been waiting for you to show up."

Again Boone shifted, shrugged. "Like I told him, that letter laid in the post office for a spell — just how long, I ain't sure."

Starbuck smiled faintly. Trevison had sidestepped the question, was neither confirming nor denying the fact that he had intended all along to sign on with Kraft as a gunman — all comments previously made notwithstanding. But he let it pass. Most of the hired guns he'd known didn't talk about their calling, and there was no reason to expect Boone to be any different. That Boone was a killer, however, would take some getting used to. He looked, talked, and acted like anything else, but that could be the secret of his effectiveness.

"Well, what do you say?"

At the sound of Trevison's voice, Shawn looked up. "Come this far, might as well go see the man," he said, raking his horse lightly with his spurs. "Can still say no if things don't suit me."

"Be up to you, of course," Trevison said, putting his bay gelding into motion. "I'm hoping you'll sign on." He hesitated, grinned self-consciously. "Sound like a wet-nose kid saying this, but I got to get it said — I ain't never met a man I felt like calling my best friend till I bumped into you. Be a fine thing if we can keep on riding together."

"Could be you're making up your mind too fast. We've only been acquainted a few hours."

"Know that, but I'm the kind that decides things quick. Didn't take me long to see that we'd make a good team."

Shawn stared off across the hills, said nothing. He'd been a loner since the day he'd ridden away from the farm on the Muskingum to begin the search for his brother. Having someone siding him continually would be a new experience — one he was not certain he could adjust to.

He needed to be free, able to move on anytime the urge came to him, halt when he wished, camp where he pleased — even hole up in some hotel, or perhaps a saloon, if it suited his mood and fancy. Having a partner could change all of that, and Shawn wasn't ready to surrender that much of his way of life as yet. He had already devoted a sizable portion of it to fulfilling Hiram Starbuck's request that he find his brother, Ben; it seemed only fair that he be permitted a few personal prerogatives.

More than once he'd been warned by interested persons with whom he'd become friendly that he could be wasting away his life on a hopeless quest, that one day he'd become aware that the years were all behind him and that it was too late to think of a future. Starbuck realized such words were only too true, but he could not turn aside, his sense of responsibility ruling out all consideration of his own needs until he had satisfied his father's wishes.

He'd not tell Boone Trevison flat out that a partnership was not for him, however. It seemed to mean much to the man, although how he could have arrived so quickly at his desire was hard to understand. Usually months, even years went into the making of a solid friendship; but Boone was different — Shawn was already realizing that . . . He'd just let the proposition hang, go unsettled. If they both went to work for Kraft, they'd be riding together, anyway.

But Trevison was unwilling to let it drop. "You like the idea?"

Starbuck shook his head. "Never was any hand to tie up with anybody for long," he said. "But if we sign up at High Green, we can see how it works out."

Boone lapsed into silence, and Shawn turned his attention to the valley stretching out before them as they dropped off the hogback. Kraft's ranch was now visible, a collection of buildings lying at the base of a high bluff a distance to their right.

Everything looked to be well cared for. The main house and the lesser structures appeared to have been only recently painted; the corrals were orderly and in good repair; and the nearby land, thick with grass and dotted with trees, ran out to all directions. A stream, the one he'd noted earlier coursing down from higher levels, cut a silver gash along the foot of the bluff and adjacent slope, while numerous ditch tributaries led from it to form stock-watering ponds as well as provide a source of supply for use of the ranch.

Small jags of cattle were scattered down the valley, but the main part of High Green range would lie farther below — where they had encountered Hugh Dixon and the other riders, Shawn guessed. And there could be even more Kraft holdings to the north as well as beyond the mountain to the west. Aaron Kraft had to be a very wealthy man; with so lush an empire, he couldn't avoid it.

They reached the yard fronting the main house and entered. Starbuck could see a neatly arranged vegetable garden, tightly fenced, forming a square below the structure, and on farther, several men were working around one of the pole corrals.

"Expect we'll find Kraft at his house," Boone said, angling toward the hitchrack and pulling to a halt. "I'll try knocking on the door, see if we can raise him."

Starbuck nodded, but he had his doubts. Aaron Kraft had not built a fine ranch like High Green from a rocking chair; it would have taken, and still require, his every waking hour. Shawn's thoughts came to a stop as the door opened. Trevison, about to swing off his saddle, caught himself, settled back, his gaze on a young woman stepping out onto the porch.

She glanced coolly from Trevison to Starbuck, allowed her attention to remain on the latter. "You're him, I suppose," she said in an icy tone.

Not tall, but well shaped, with light-blue eyes and a wealth of dark, silky hair gathered on top of her head and flowing down around her neck, she presented an attractive if somewhat hostile picture standing there in the streaming sunlight.

"I'm who?" Shawn asked, removing his hat.

"The gunman Pa — my father — sent for, Boone Trevison."

Starbuck smiled. "Afraid not. He's Trevison."

A frown crossed the even features of Aaron Kraft's daughter, and something akin to surprise filled her wide-set eyes.

"You?" she said, shifting her attention.

Boone smiled. "Yes'm, I'm Trevison. Like to talk to your pa."

Still frowning, the girl half-turned, pointed toward the corral, where Shawn had noticed several men had gathered.

"You'll find him down there," she said. "They're breaking some horses today."

"Thank you, ma'am," Trevison said, touching the brim of his hat with a forefinger, but the girl had abruptly wheeled and was re-entering the house.

CHAPTER
SEVEN

Pulling away, Starbuck and Boone Trevison circled the house and rode slowly across the hardpack lying between it and the structures to the west. All things were in place, well kept, and the barren ground had the appearance of having been swept. Large cottonwoods, strategically arranged, spread thickly leafed limbs overhead, providing ample shade for the area.

A man holding a pitchfork stood in the wide doorway of the barn. He considered them briefly and then turned back to whatever duties he was performing inside the bulky building. Nearby two riders were dozing on a bench built against what evidently was the bunkhouse. They would be part of the night crew, taking their ease, Shawn reckoned.

They reached the edge of the yard, entered an alleyway between a wagonshed and an open-sided, roofed-over affair in which hay was stacked, and slanted toward a corral where the men were gathered. The solid thud of hooves, shouts, clouds of spinning dust, and the squeak of leather bore out the girl's words that horses were in the process of being broken to the saddle at that hour.

The dozen or so riders, some hanging on the heavy horizontal poles that made up the enclosure, others perched on the top, turned to look as Starbuck and Boone rode up. Immediately a squat, ruddy-complexioned man separated himself from the group.

"Trevison?" he asked, coming forward.

"That's me," Boone said heartily, pulling the bay to a halt. "You Mr. Kraft?"

"Took you long enough," the rancher said, not bothering to answer the question. "Who's he?"

"My partner. Name's Shawn Starbuck. Letter of yours said there'd be work —"

"Know what I said," Kraft grumbled impatiently.

Aaron Kraft looked to be anything but a wealthy cattle grower. His pants were old and stained, his boots scuffed and badly run down at the heels. The drab gray shirt he wore was collarless and closed at the neck with a copper button.

"Let's go up to the house. Like to do my talking over a cup of coffee," he said, and without glancing back, started across the hardpack.

Starbuck and Trevison, still on the saddle, trailed the rancher to a rack built at the edge of the yard, halted, and dismounting, followed him up onto the porch that extended across the rear of the structure. A table with several straight-backed chairs occupied its center, and motioning for them to be seated, Aaron Kraft stepped up to an inner door.

"Leda!" he shouted. "Can use some coffee out here. There's three of us."

44

Dropping back to the table, the rancher settled down, brushed at the sweat on his face and balding pate.

"Leda's my daughter," he explained. "Expect you met her when you rode in — or did you come straight back?"

"We talked to her," Boone said, and glanced up as the door opened and the girl appeared.

In one hand she carried a mid-size granite pot, in the other several tin cups — four, to be exact, Shawn noted. Evidently Kraft's daughter intended to sit in on the conversation.

"Trevison says you've met," Kraft said in his gruff, hard-edged way.

Leda distributed the cups, nodded at Shawn. "Didn't get his name."

"Starbuck — he's Trevison's partner," Kraft explained, hooking a finger in the handle of his cup. "They work together, I reckon."

The girl said nothing as she filled the cups, including one for herself, and then sank onto a chair. Shawn gave her name thought: *Leda*. He'd never heard it before. Likely it had some family origin.

"We ain't much on drinking around here, but I expect we can scare you up something to put in your coffee, if you want it," Kraft said.

Starbuck waved the offer aside. Trevison said, "Coffee'll be fine like it is."

Kraft's thick shoulders stirred. "Well, I reckon we'd best get down to business," he said, taking a sip of the steaming black liquid. "I'll start at the bottom, let you know just what it's all about and what I'm expecting you to do."

Shawn placed his attention on the rancher. He knew the answer to his question before asking, but he wanted to hear it said.

"It going to be something besides regular cowhand work?"

Kraft snorted. "Cowhands! Hell's fire, they come a dime a dozen. Can get all I want —"

"Problem's keeping them," Leda murmured.

"I'll come to that in due time," the rancher snapped testily. "First you got to know this — I'm the biggest man in the country, biggest in more ways than you'd ever guess. I own forty thousand acres of the finest grassland God ever put on this earth, and I've built up the best damned ranch that you or anybody else has ever seen. On top of that, I'm the richest man in the territory, and can do pretty well as I please.

"Cattle buyers all over the country are begging to buy my beef and are ready to pay top price — my price, it usually turns out to be. I sell my stock in Denver. Drive my herds through the mountains on a trail I built myself.

"Now, maybe that all sounds like Texas brag, but it ain't. It's true. Built all this up myself in the last twenty-some-odd years, asking no favors from nobody, and took my luck however it came — good or bad — and licked it.

"Never tromped on nobody's toes doing it. I treated every man I dealt with honest and fair and made them treat me the same way . . . That's one thing that's made

46

me big as I am — being on the square, no matter what the deal was."

Aaron Kraft paused for breath. Starbuck considered him quietly. The rancher had a hard, abrasive manner, likely could count the number of friends he had on one hand. That he was proud of his achievements to the point of rank conceit was evident, but he reckoned a man with such success, as was evident to the eye, could be forgiven that shortcoming — if he didn't subvert it into a tool with which to harass his neighbors.

Shawn slid a glance at Leda. Her features were expressionless, seeming neither to approve nor to disprove, verify or deny the claims of her parent. He looked then to Trevison. Boone was listening intently, absorbing it all, word by word.

Down at the breaking corral shouts were going up as something of note occurred, and over in front of the barn two men were now rolling out a buckboard and pointing it for a shed with an extended canopy-like roof under which was a forge and other smithy equipment.

Aaron Kraft's voice broke the space of quiet that had settled over the porch, began to drone on again. Starbuck only half-listened as the rancher recounted the hardships he'd endured in his early days on the Packsaddles: the severe winters that all but wiped out his small herds; the marauding Indians; droughts, unsuspected in that part of the country; the problems with rustlers, outlaws, and greedy politicians.

It was one man's story of his own success, undoubtedly merited, but the gist of it had an all too familiar ring — a big rancher wanting to become even bigger, and willing to pay the price to attain that goal. Shawn stirred. He'd been that road before, too, and he was equally unsure if he wanted to ride it again . . . Far off to the north three gunshots echoed hollowly in quick succession. That, somehow, seemed to be a sign, a warning of things to come.

". . . that there's the problem — they're all working to drive me out."

Starbuck drew to attention, the last of the rancher's words registering on his consciousness.

"What was that?" he asked.

Aaron Kraft considered him sourly. "Ain't you paying no attention?"

"Expect I'm hearing what's necessary," Shawn replied quietly.

Trevison shifted nervously on his chair, and a faint smile had broken the firm set of Leda Kraft's lips, while a small light began to dance in her eyes.

"I didn't quite get the last of what you were saying . . ."

"Well, damnit, Starbuck, clean out your ears!" the rancher snapped. "Ain't no hand at chewing my cabbage twice . . . What I said was that my neighbors've all lined themselves up against me and are aiming to run me out."

Shawn leaned back. "Was what I thought you said, only I figured maybe I'd heard wrong. Usually the

48

other way around — big rancher gobbling up the little ones."

"That ain't how it is here," Kraft said, his irritation fading. "And if I don't do something fast to stop it, they're sure going to get it done."

CHAPTER
EIGHT

The silence that followed Aaron Kraft's words was broken only by the sounds at the corral, where wranglers were working with the mustangs. Finally Starbuck spoke.

"When'd all this start?"

"Been about a year. They —"

"Who're they?"

"Loudmouth named Ford Lalicker heads up the bunch. His place is on up the flat a piece — on the north line of my property, in fact. Next to him's Dave Wescott. They back up against the mountains, same as I do. Then, there's Saul Bradley — runs the Box B outfit. He's out on the flats, east of here. Eric McCroden's another'n. His place is south of town. Right below him's Carl Mayberry."

"What set you to thinking they want to drive you out?" Trevison asked.

"Well, now, if you was finding your water holes salted, your cattle drove off a bluff and killed, your line shacks set afire, and your hired hands shot at pretty regular like, wouldn't you figure something was going on?"

Boone nodded soberly. "Reckon I would."

"Been rustling, too, but a man big as me's got to sort of expect that, and I don't mind it much if I know some of my beef's going to fill the bellies of a hungry hayshaker and his family. Stealing just to spite me's something else, however, and like all the rest of the devilment going on, it's got to stop — even if it takes some killing to do it."

"You got a full crew now?" Starbuck wondered.

"Pretty much. Getting hard to hire on help to replace the men that've turned tail and quit, though. Can't say as I blame them much — forty a month and found ain't a lot when you have to be dodging bushwhackers' bullets."

"These other ranchers you mentioned — are they making it all right — successful, I mean?"

"Far as I know. Things ain't as good out on the flats as they are along the mountains — I got better grass and more water — but I reckon you could say they're all plenty well off."

"Then what's the argument all about? You tell us they want to break you, drive you out of the country; got to be a reason why."

"Envy, that's what! Ain't nothing but pure envy . . . and fear."

Fear . . . Starbuck nodded slowly, a glimmer of understanding beginning to break through. Fear, in one form or another, was the basis for just about all of the trouble he'd encountered in his wanderings across the frontier.

"Fear of what?"

Kraft raised both hands, allowed them to drop in a gesture of frustration.

"They've got some fool notion that I'm wanting their land — specially Lalicker and Dave Westcott, them being right north of me."

"But you don't —"

"Hell, no! Got more land now than I can use. You just ask my foreman, Lige Hathaway, or any of the boys riding for me — they'll tell you we don't graze no more'n three-quarters of my range. Rest just stands there growing and waiting to be used."

Shawn moved his empty cup toward Leda Kraft. The girl had remained utterly silent except for her remarks at the beginning of the conversation.

"Something must've started this Lalicker and the others thinking the way they do," he said thoughtfully.

Unconsciously he reached up, explored the tenderness on the side of his face. He was becoming aware now of other places on his body — sore reminders of the encounter with Ford Lalicker's hired hands.

Kraft rubbed at his jaw, watched his daughter refill the cups all around. Once he shifted his eyes to the bruised area of Starbuck's cheek, but he made no comment on it.

"Only thing I can recollect is that homesteader I had some dealings with a few years back," he said after a time. "Fellow had a hundred and sixty acres laying between me and Lalicker. Thing about it was that it blocked the trail I was driving my cattle to Denver on. Had to swing wide to miss his land . . . and that of

Lalicker's. Matter of around a hundred rough extra miles before it was done with.

"Figured the only answer was to buy out this Keeling — that was the sodbuster's name. He didn't much want to sell, and I sort of had to talk him into it. Wasn't no chousing him around, understand, but I did have to keep after him, him being one of them no-accounts — the kind that's too lazy to holler sooey when the hogs are after them.

"Finally bought him out — at his price, which was a hell of a lot more'n it should've been, and ten times what he put into it. But having that piece of property so's I could save that hundred miles was important to me. I figure it was worth it."

"And you figure Lalicker thinks you're out to get his land, and Wescott's too, since their places adjoin yours."

"That's how I see it."

"Where do the ranchers out on the flats come in?"

"Ford's done a lot of talking to them, got them believing that once I lay my hands on his and Wescott's ranges, I'll start after theirs."

"You ever come right out and talk to them, tell them there's nothing to what Lalicker says?"

Kraft wagged his head. "Tried. Paid calls on them all, made it plain I didn't want their damned ranches, that I had more'n I could manage. Even got the preacher to let me get up one Sunday in church and speak my piece. Most of them was there, but it didn't do no good. Very next day we found a half-dozen steers laying in a gully on the east range. Been shot through the heads.

"That's when I started thinking about hiring on somebody to look after my interests. Lalicker had put on a couple of hardcases — three of them, to be exact — that were crowding my boys, making it tough for them to do their jobs. Only way I could see to buck that was get my own gunslinger, turn him loose."

"Which I still believe is the wrong way to go about it," Leda said, at last breaking her silence with a disapproval. "There's certain to be a better way."

"Then what is it?" Kraft shot back impatiently. "You tell me what it is, and if it's something I ain't already tried, I'll sure's hell take a stab at it!"

The girl's shoulders stirred. "I . . . I don't know, but this seems wrong to me, turning hired" — she paused, glanced at Starbuck and Boone Trevison with no apology in her eyes — "killers loose to deal with people who are our friends."

"Were," the rancher corrected bluntly. "Ain't a one of them can be called that now — or for quite a time, if you're being truthful. Anyway, I ain't doing nothing that Ford Lalicker hasn't done. He brought in gunslingers, didn't he — that Charlie Vine and Bill Bristol and Al whatever-his-name-is. They're responsible for all the trouble we're having now — every last bit of it. Already drove off four or five of my riders. Like as not they'll try running you two off . . ."

"Already have," Boone drawled. "Seen them when we first rode into town. We made it plain we'd not be moving on."

Kraft grinned broadly at Trevison. "Yocum told me I could depend on you — he's that cattle buyer that give me your name and where I could write you. Said if I could hire you on, my problems was over. I'm beginning to think he was right, but I'm going to be honest and tell you I sort of had my doubts when I first set eyes on you. You ain't exactly what I was expecting you to look like."

Shawn stared off across the yard. He'd gotten the same impression, but evidently Boone Trevison was well known and highly respected in circles where men of his calling were found. For a cattle buyer, a person who visited the country widely and dealt with men who had use for a hired gun, to recommend Boone was uncontestable proof of his ability.

But Starbuck was giving only a small amount of thought to that matter; the reason why rancher Ford Lalicker and others in the Packsaddle country had turned against Kraft still puzzled him. It appeared to him the rancher was honest and sincere — if somewhat overbearing and inclined to excessive pride — and that he had made every effort to ease the tension that now gripped the country.

What else could lie behind Lalicker's activities? Was there some deep reason, something everyone, including the other ranchers, was missing? Was Ford Lalicker using fear as a tool to gain his own ends? If so, what was it the man wanted? Was he just out to get High Green for himself?

"Reckon that there gives you the story, just the way it is," he heard Aaron Kraft say. "I'm tired of the way things are going, and I want you to put a stop to it. All

I'm looking to do is run my ranch, raise and sell cattle the way I like to — the way I been doing.

"One of these here days I expect this girl of mine to hitch up with a good man and give me some grandchildren. I'm hoping and planning to leave them a fine ranch to take over when I'm gone."

"Can't see as there'll be any big problem," Boone said quietly. "How far you want me to go?"

The rancher glanced at his daughter, shrugged. "Far as you like. If it takes killing to get it settled, then killing it'll have to be."

Trevison nodded, turned to Starbuck. "Guess that lays it out plain enough. But it's more'n a one-man job. I'm ready to take it on if my partner here'll side me. What do you say, Shawn? You dealing yourself in?"

CHAPTER
NINE

Idly Starbuck sloshed the contents of his cup about. "Some men don't mind being called a gunslinger. I do — mostly because I'm not one," he said after a time. "On top of that, I've had about all the shooting I can take for a spell. Not sure I want to get mixed up in something like this."

"Said you could use a job," Trevison observed.

"Nothing new to that. Happens plenty often, and I don't ever do much worrying over it. Work always turns up."

"It's turned up right here and now," Aaron Kraft said, nodding. "And I'm willing to pay good."

"Expect you are," Shawn murmured, eyes on several men riding into the yard and pulling up in front of the bunkhouse.

"Then what's the problem? You figure the odds are all wrong?"

Starbuck's shoulders stirred. Odds had nothing to do with it. He'd lined up with plenty of other outfits in the past where the chances for coming out with a whole skin were much worse than here on Aaron Kraft's High Green. It was simply that he did not fully understand just what it was all about.

He continued to ask himself why the smaller ranchers wanted to drive out a man who apparently had not harmed them and had no intention of doing so in the future. Envy hardly seemed reason enough, nor did jealousy. What, then, was it all about?

"Sure would be obliged to you, Shawn, if you'd stick with me," Boone said earnestly. "It'll be a mite tough for me to go it alone."

Starbuck smiled faintly. He still hadn't figured out the gunman, either. Boone, it seemed to him, was long on taking credit but a bit short on doing anything when the moment required. It would be worth something to see how he reacted when a moment of truth presented itself . . . That, added to the puzzle of why Aaron Kraft was being persecuted, did heighten his interest in the situation considerably.

"Be worth two hundred dollars a month to you," Kraft said, "and I ain't against paying a little bonus on the side when the job's done. You come a mite higher," he added, nodding to Trevison. "I understand that. Yocum said it'd take five hundred dollars to hire you on. That's jake with me, and the bonus goes for you, too."

"Sure is good money," Boone said wistfully. "What do you say, Shawn? You with me? Can't do no better'n that, far as wages are concerned."

Starbuck smiled. "Twice that much's not enough to get killed for, but I'll string along — leastwise, for a month or two."

Trevison slapped the tabletop jubilantly with the palms of his hands. The tin cups jumped from the impact.

"Fine! Fine! Won't be no job a'tall getting this mess straightened out for Mr. Kraft."

"As soon you'd call me Aaron," the rancher said.

"All right, Aaron it'll be. And I'm Boone, and Starbuck there is Shawn — and I reckon we're ready to go to work."

Kraft bobbed, said, "Guess we're ready to get down to business, then . . . How about some more of that java, girl?"

The pot was empty. Leda, silent as before, got to her feet, and carrying it into the kitchen, apparently refilled it from a larger container that was kept simmering on the back of the stove.

When she had returned and was pouring the cups full again, Kraft said, "What's going to be your first move? Like to know, so's I can figure what I ought, or ought not, to be doing."

Trevison frowned, leaned back in his chair. "Well, I reckon there's two, maybe three things we can start right off, it all depending . . . Shawn, what's your idea?"

Starbuck studied the gunman over the rim of his cup as he sipped at the black coffee. "You're the man calling the shots. I'll leave it up to you."

"Know that, and I'm obliged, but we're together in this, and you're entitled to a say-so."

"It's you that's had the most experience."

Kraft swore explosively. "What the hell's all this polite business?" he demanded. "I'll be thinking neither one of you knows what's to be done if you keep on swapping it back and forth like you're doing!"

59

Trevison laughed. "Expect that maybe's what it sounds like, but me and him are partners, and I want to be sure we're thinking the same things. It's real important that we do at a time like this. Now, if you've got a plan, Shawn, let's hear it. Want to see if it matches up with what I've got in mind."

Starbuck returned his cup to the table, shifted on his chair. "Way I'd start off would be to take a ride back to town this evening, show up in that saloon . . ."

"The Cattleking?" Kraft wondered.

"Yeh, seemed to be the biggest, so it'll have the best crowd. I'd serve notice that I was hiring out to High Green and aimed to put an end to all the things that were happening to it — the burnings and slaughter of cattle, and people taking potshots at the ranchhands, and so on.

"I'd lay it on plenty strong, not leave any doubt that I meant business and that any man caught on High Green range who didn't belong there was as good as dead."

"Just exactly what I was thinking!" Boone Trevison said approvingly. "And I'd tell them from now on I'll be shooting first and asking questions later. Pretty sure that'd change things around here."

"Need to say that if something happened on High Green range and the men responsible weren't caught right at that time, they'd be tracked down and made to pay for what they did, along with whoever hired them to do it," Starbuck finished.

"Sounds good to me," Aaron Kraft said, nodding. "Especially that last. You grab some of them jaspers shooting my cattle and burning my line shacks, and make them talk, you'll mighty quick find out who's behind all the trouble. Not that I don't already know, but you'll have proof then, I mean."

"Which is when you need to go to the law," Leda said quietly. "Taking it into your own hands won't help. That will only keep this . . . this feud going."

"Stringing up a couple of them gunslingers to the nearest tree'll help aplenty!" Kraft declared hotly. "Law! What the hell could old John Coon do? Fire went out in his stove a long time ago."

"He's still the law, and it's a matter for him to handle."

"The lady's right," Starbuck said. "Have to give him a chance to do something about it, once we've got clear proof. If he doesn't, then's the time to try something else."

"Way I see it, too," Boone said.

The rancher turned his attention to the gunman, viewed him thoughtfully while he scrubbed at his stubble of beard with thick fingers. Shouts were coming from the breaking corral, and over behind the barn a dog was barking frantically.

"Well, maybe so," Kraft said finally. "I'm putting it in your hands, since I'm paying you to do what's needful. Never could see the sense in hiring a man to do a job, then not letting him do it."

"Just you rest easy, Aaron," Trevison said reassuringly. "Me and Shawn'll see to everything. Don't you fret no more about it."

"Don't aim to," the rancher said flatly, and drew himself upright. "Expect you can use a little advance on your wages — ain't run across a hand yet that wasn't flat broke, or near to it . . . Come on into my office and do some signing up — always like to put things down in writing, so's there won't be no misunderstandings — and I'll fork over a bit of cash."

"Sure thing," Trevison said, rising, and smiling at Leda, followed the rancher into the house.

"Coffee's cold again," the girl said. "Would you like for me to get some more?"

"Obliged," Starbuck replied, "but I've had enough." He grinned, looked at her more closely. "For a woman, you don't talk much."

Leda's brows lifted. "Not sure if I'm to take that as a compliment or not! But I guess that's my way. I learned long ago that it's useless to argue with my father. You just can't come out ahead, so I keep quiet . . . Not much of a talker yourself."

"Depends on the company — and the time."

"I thought that was probably it. Your friend more than makes up for you, however."

"He's real handy with words, all right."

"I'm a little surprised at Papa. He usually backs away from the ones who aren't pretty closemouthed . . . One thing I'll give you credit for, you didn't ask me where I got a name like Leda. Most everyone else does."

Starbuck smiled again. "With a name like Shawn, I'm not about to question what someone else's called!"

62

"Have to admit I did wonder about it. My name comes from the old Greek legends, something my mother, who was a schoolteacher, liked to read and talk about. Leda was the mother of Helen of Troy. Mother liked the name and gave it to me when I was born."

"About the same story where I'm concerned. My mother, Clare, was a teacher too. Worked among the Shawnee Indians. She shortened the word into a name for me when I came along. Your mother around somewhere?"

"No, she's back east visiting relatives — has been there for about a year, in fact, and probably won't return for a few more months. Mother doesn't like it very well here — just never could get used to it, I guess. Were you born in this part of the country?"

"No, in Ohio. Been knocking around the West for several years, though. You must have spent some time back east yourself, judging from the way you talk."

Shawn was finding Leda Kraft pleasant company and was enjoying his conversation with her, as she evidently was with him.

"My mother insisted on it — that I go to school there, I mean. I was sent to live with relatives in New York when I was six years old. Traveled back and forth every spring and fall, attending school there in the winter, spending my summers here on the ranch."

Starbuck glanced to the kitchen door. A heavyset red-faced woman had appeared, was standing in the oblong opening looking off across the road. Apparently the Kraft cook and housekeeper, he guessed. Leda did not trouble to glance around.

"Expect you got pretty well acquainted with railroads and stagecoaches, doing that," he said.

Leda's lips curled slightly at the thought. "So much so that I'm sick of both," she said. "After I had completed twelve grades, I went to a girls' finishing school for two years. That was the end of it for me. When it was over, I returned here and stayed. I'd had all the education I wanted."

Leda paused, her long, slender fingers, which seemingly would be more in place at the keyboard of a spinet or some such other variation of artistic endeavor than handling the reins of a horse, toying with an empty cup.

"Do you think you'll ever return to Ohio?" she asked after a time.

"Not to stay," Shawn replied. "My folks are both dead, and the farm where my brother and I were born has been sold. Only kind of life I want is here in this country."

"Life . . . as a gunfighter?"

"Not my calling — already mentioned that. Just sort of fell into this job."

"What did you do — your calling, as you term it?"

"Nothing special. I've done about everything. Teamster, lawman, freight skinner, cowhand, wagon-train scout. Rode shotgun on a train up in Kansas for a few months once, did the same on an ore wagon down around Tombstone — a town in Arizona Territory — not too long ago."

"I'd say you're not too much at staying put," the girl observed, a fine edge of disapproval in her tone.

He shrugged. "Yeh, reckon you could say that."

"Well, I hope you stay around here for a while," Leda said, boldly frank, and then added, "Not for any reason except to get things cleared up for Papa. Everything he told you is the gospel truth."

Shawn nodded. "Figured it was."

"He's an honest man. Never cheated anyone in his life, and he's always tried to get along with other people. I'm not telling you this just because he's my father, but because I want you to know he wasn't lying to you. He never does — or has — not to anybody."

Starbuck made no comment. Then: "A bit hard for me to understand what's causing all the trouble for him. If he's what you say he is, and I sure believe you, why are Lalicker and the others so dead-set on pulling him down?"

"Ford Lalicker's at the bottom of it. He's got the others listening to him . . . and it goes back a long way, to the time before I was born and Papa was settling the place."

Shawn centered his attention on the girl. Her eyes, the blue even brighter in the flooding sunlight, were intense, as if she were remembering all the problems that had beset her father and was resenting mightily each and every one. She was very like Aaron Kraft in her beliefs and love for High Green but had none of her mother's desire to spend time elsewhere.

"Ford Lalicker came here about the same time. He was looking for land where he could build a ranch too. They both scouted this area, but Papa was the first to claim it. Lalicker has never forgotten, or forgiven, for that. He had to settle for land north of us, second best, you might say, but it's still a fine piece of property. He's done real well there."

"Then it's just your pa getting this place — High Green — instead of him that's at the bottom of the problem. It's been sticking in his craw all these years, finally got to gnawing at him so hard that he decided to do something about it. Can you think of any other reason than that?"

"None," Leda said promptly. "Ford Lalicker's made a lot of money on the Maple Leaf — that's what he calls his ranch."

"Not much of a reason to kill or get killed for," Shawn murmured.

"Just what I told Papa when I was trying to talk him out of sending for Boone Trevison. But Lalicker had brought in gunfighters, and they were starting to cause trouble for us . . . I guess he really didn't have much choice."

Starbuck swore grimly under his breath. An old wheeze hammered into his and Ben's heads by their father when they were small filled his mind. *An idle mind is the devil's workshop*, it ran. And trite as it was, it applied to Ford Lalicker. Successful, well off, with all the trials and tribulations of getting his ranch started and doing well behind him, he had nothing to do but think back to old wrongs, fancied or otherwise, and take steps to right them.

"Somebody good at talking ought to get with this Lalicker, make him see what he's stirring up."

"That's been tried," Leda said wearily. "Not only by Papa, but by others — the minister of our church, several of the town's merchants where we do our trading, even Marshal Coon. It hasn't done any good. Nobody can make Ford Lalicker realize what this can turn into. He's taken it into his head to get High Green, even if he causes a lot of blood to be spilled."

"Just how it's going to end up. The town merchants — folks like that — where do they stand? Are they taking sides?"

"They're just sort of staying out of it, waiting, you might say. When it's all over, they don't want to have been on the losing side."

That was understandable, if deplorable. The businessmen of Carsonville derived a livelihood from the ranchers in the Packsaddle country; it was only prudent not to become strongly identified with either of the factions embroiled in the struggle.

Shawn started to say more, hesitated, glanced to the kitchen door. Aaron Kraft, with Trevison at his heels, stepped out onto the porch and moved toward the table.

"Can start your doings anytime," the rancher said, flipping a double eagle to Starbuck. "You're on my payroll beginning right now."

CHAPTER
TEN

Starbuck caught the gold coin, nodded. "Obliged," he said, and dropping it into a pocket of his shirt, got to his feet.

"Can put your gear in that cabin over there next the cook shack," Kraft continued, pointing to a small, pitched-roof structure at the edge of the hardpack. "My foreman used to live in it — him and his wife. She died a while back, and he moved into the bunkhouse with the rest of the crew. Said it was too lonesome there by himself."

"Be fine," Trevison said, his attention again on Leda. That he was attracted to the girl was evident, but it was equally plain she had little time for him.

"Do your eating with us here in the house," the rancher went on. "Wife's away, so there's only me and the girl."

"Suits me," Boone said quickly, and then frowned as Shawn shook his head. "What's wrong with that? We've got to eat."

"If it's all the same," Starbuck explained, "I'll take my meals with the crew — not that I wouldn't enjoy the company," he added, smiling at Leda, "but on this kind of a job, a man needs to know what's going on all the time. Best place to get it is from the hands that are out on the range or spending time in town."

Trevison shrugged. "Don't see that we need to —"

"No reason why you should pass up the offer," Starbuck cut in, recognizing the gunman's reluctance. "One of us hanging around the crew will be enough."

Trevison grinned broadly. "Expect you're right."

He was pleased with the arrangement, but no more so than Shawn, who was not anxious to spend any more time with Aaron Kraft — or his daughter — than necessary. Too close an association with either, especially the girl, could lead to complications. Whether Boone Trevison realized that or not, and he showed little indication of such, they were taking on a job involving considerable danger, and one that would require their complete attention.

"I expect you ought to meet some of the boys first off, so's they'll know who you are," Kraft said, moving down off the porch and starting across the hardpack for the crew's quarters. "Most of them're out on the range this time of day, but there's a few that was working close enough to come in for a bite of lunch."

Leda had turned away, gone into the house. Shawn, following the rancher, slowed to allow Boone to catch up. The gunman was smiling.

"Going to like this job," he murmured.

Starbuck hitched up the gun on his hip. "Yeh, only thing we need do is stay alive," he said dryly.

"Oh, doubt if we'll be taking any chances. Aaron tells me nobody's got shot yet, just scared off."

"That'll change now, with us going to work for him," Shawn said, and halted as they reached the sprawling bunkhouse.

Two men were lounging on a bench placed against the front of the low-roofed structure. A third slouched in its doorway.

"Lige," Kraft said, "like for you to meet a couple of new hands."

The older of the pair on the bench rose, ambled forward. In his early forties, he had thick, dark hair and small, buttonlike eyes.

"Howdy. I'm pleased to meet you," he said with an unmistakable Texas accent as he extended a hand to Boone.

"He's Trevison," Kraft explained. "Reckon you heard me talking about him. Partner there is Starbuck . . . Lige — rest of his name's Hathaway — is my foreman."

Hathaway's attitude changed visibly. "I'm mighty glad you've showed up," he said, turning from Trevison to Shawn. "We're sure needing a little of your kind of help." He paused, pointed to the man still sitting on the bench. "That there's my brother, Joe. Fellow standing in the doorway is Dan Chesser."

Both riders nodded in the reserved, noncommittal way of cowhands greeting strangers. Kraft rubbed his palms together, glanced about.

"Anybody else around?"

Hathaway said, "Nope, 'cepting the night boys, and they're sleeping. Rest've all rode back out. Couple or three of them wranglers down at the breaking corral, maybe."

70

"No bother. Trevison and Starbuck can shake their hands later. Now, Starbuck'll be taking his meals with you and the others, Trevison's eating with me. I'm putting them up in your old house . . . Want you to spread the word, Lige, about them getting here — finally. Reckon everybody knows what they come for."

"For certain," the foreman agreed in his lazy, easygoing manner.

"Don't want nobody getting in their way. They're riding into town late this afternoon or this evening to get things squared off. Probably be smart was you to send somebody out, tell the boys they ain't strangers, so's they won't be stopping them. Trevison here'll be riding that bay over there, and Starbuck's forking the sorrel."

"Can send Dan out," Hathaway said, glancing at Chesser. "He come in saying he felt poorly. Don't think he's hurting so bad he can't do that."

Kraft turned to Boone Trevison. "There anything else I ought to be doing to get you set?"

The gunman shook his head. "Nope, not far as I can figure."

The rancher bobbed. "Well, I'll leave you to your moving in. Anything more that needs hashing over, we can do at supper."

Aaron Kraft turned on a heel, struck for the main house. Shawn put his attention on Lige Hathaway.

"There a chance the cook can come up with a bite of lunch for us? Been a long time since breakfast — and it wasn't much."

"Sure thing," the foreman replied, pointing at the cookhouse. "Right over there. His name's Hobie. Just tell him I said to feed you."

About an hour before sunset, Starbuck, with Boone Trevison at his side, rode out of High Green and headed down the road for Carsonville. They had moved their gear, such as it was, into the shack once occupied by Lige Hathaway, enjoyed a good noonday meal grumpily furnished by the elderly Hobie, who complained continually about being compelled to feed the help at all hours, and met a few more of Aaron Kraft's crew.

"Sure think I'm going to like this here job," Trevison said, again expressing his pleasure as they loped along the road. "They're mighty fine folks, them Krafts. He's maybe a little bit mouthy when it comes to talking about himself, but I reckon we ought to overlook that, it being true mostly what he says . . . And that daughter of his — she's something, ain't she?"

Shawn nodded absently. He'd seen no more of Leda after their first meeting and had dismissed her from his thoughts, occupying his mind instead with the more important and necessary things pertaining to the job he had co-assumed.

"Expect you'd best do the talking when we get to the saloon," Shawn said. "Seems Kraft's pretty well bandied your name around already, sort of using it as a threat. Knowing you're here ought to have some effect."

72

"Guess it will, sure enough," Trevison agreed. Then: "You think there's a chance Lalicker will back off when he finds out Kraft's sure enough hired me — us — on?"

They had topped out the hogback, were dropping over onto the opposite side. Starbuck swept the slope below them with a probing glance, saw nothing to disturb him.

"From what I've heard about him, I doubt it. It's gone too far, for one thing, and he's evidently a proud man, same as Kraft. Seems Lalicker's got a big hate burning inside him — started when Kraft beat him to the land he wanted. Guess it's finally boiled over, and he won't quit now until it's satisfied."

"Where'd you hear all that? Never heard Aaron mention it."

"Came from his daughter. We did some talking while you were inside with him, signing up."

"Leda told you all that?" Trevison said, his tone slightly sharp. "What else was you — ?"

The dry crack of a pistol cut through Boone Trevison's words. He yelled, grabbed at his arm as his startled horse reared, plunged off onto the shoulder of the road.

Starbuck, throwing himself forward on the saddle to make himself as difficult a target as possible, jammed spurs into the sorrel's flanks, sent him rushing off into the brush. The shot had come — he thought — from somewhere on their right.

Weapon in hand, he whipped the gelding back and forth between the trees and clumps of brush, eyes searching ceaselessly as he sought to get a glimpse of the bushwhacker, while one fact gradually became apparent in his mind: someone knew that he and Boone were making the ride into Carsonville, had waited to ambush the gunman.

And only someone on High Green could have been aware of such, could have known they would be passing that way. Aaron Kraft had a traitor working for him — someone in the pay of Ford Lalicker whose job it was to kill High Green's gunman before he could become a threat. That knowledge struck Starbuck with full force.

Grim, he rode on, working deeper into the thick growth covering the slope, watching, listening, alert for any indication of the would-be killer's location. It was hopeless. Whoever it was had faded off into the shadowy, dense cover on the mountainside after firing a lone shot, and disappeared. He'd best get back to Boone Trevison, see how badly the gunman was wounded. Wheeling the heaving sorrel about, Starbuck returned to the road.

Trevison was still on the saddle. Shawn felt a rush of relief when he saw the man waiting off to one side at the edge of the brush.

"Glad you're not hurt," he said.

Boone grinned wryly, removed the hand he was holding to his left arm. "Ain't nothing but a scratch. Hardly drew blood. A hair more and he'd a missed me altogether. You get a look at who it was?"

"Had pulled out," Starbuck replied, settling back.

If Boone, scarcely nicked, had thought to ride onto the slope with him, taking a lower course and thus forming a two-pronged probe, they might have trapped the bushwhacker between them. But it hadn't occurred to Trevison, and Shawn, unaware of the extent of the man's wound, had given it no consideration.

"Expect we'd best head back to the ranch. I . . ." Trevison began, and checked as Starbuck raised a warning hand.

Far down on the road the quick, hollow beat of a fast-running horse was suddenly hanging in the warm, still air.

"That'll be him — let's go!" Shawn yelled, and roweling the sorrel, swung off in pursuit.

He hadn't mentioned his belief that someone working for Kraft was the bushwhacker; there hadn't been time, for one thing, and too, Trevison, with all his experience, likely had already come to the same conclusion. Later, if they failed to overtake the rider ahead of them, he'd discuss it with Boone, see if he had any ideas as to who it might be. It was just possible Trevison had seen one of High Green's hired hands ride out shortly before they did.

The slope gradually stretched out behind them as the horses raced headlong down the grade. They came to the edge of the flat, and Starbuck, raising himself in the stirrups, endeavored to catch sight of the man they were following. It wasn't possible. Darkness, combining with the many bends in the road, the clumps of brush, and scatters of small trees, closed off all view except for a short distance ahead.

Shawn slowed the sorrel to a fair lope, glanced at Trevison, drawing alongside. "Might as well ease off.

He'll reach town before we can overhaul him. Best bet now's to have a look around when we get there."

Boone nodded, his lean face sober in the murky dusk. "That was one of Lalicker's bunch — had to be. Was just setting there, waiting, aiming to pick me off."

"Was what he figured to do," Shawn agreed, gaze now on the lights of the settlement, winking through the night from a mile distant.

Evidently the possibility that there was a traitor working for Aaron Kraft hadn't occurred to the gunman. Starbuck frowned. Maybe he was reaching a bit, jumping at such a conclusion; he'd best keep the idea to himself until he could turn up more proof, one way or another.

"You still planning to lay out your warning?" he asked minutes later when they turned onto the town's main street and pointed for the Cattleking.

Trevison brushed at his mouth. "You think I ought to, after . . . after whoever that was took a shot at me?"

"Can't see as that makes any difference . . . maybe makes it more necessary than ever," Starbuck replied, and then added dryly, "Was what we rode down here for, anyway."

CHAPTER
ELEVEN

"Around back," Starbuck said as they approached the saloon.

"Plenty of room right here in front," Trevison said protestingly, gesturing at the dozen or more horses lined up at the hitchrack at the edge of the street.

"Can see that. Figured it'd be smart to have a look at things first, however . . . and I'd as soon we'd keep in the dark when we get ready to leave, too."

Boone grunted his agreement, swung his bay in behind Starbuck's sorrel as the tall rider turned in alongside the building and pointed for the deeply shadowed area in the rear.

There was an equal number of horses standing at the rack there, and pulling up to its end, Shawn halted, dismounted. Trevison was close by. Wheeling immediately, Starbuck began to work his way along the slack-hipped animals, slipping a hand under their saddle blankets. When he had finished, Boone was waiting for him.

"Anything?"

"All cold," Starbuck replied. "I'll take a look at the ones out front."

"You figure you might find the nag that bushwhacker was riding — that it?"

"Slim chance, but worth going to the trouble. Expect whoever it was would've left his horse somewhere else if he aimed to come here. Probably knew this is where we were headed."

As he anticipated, none of the mounts stationed at the hitchrack on the street was still hot and sweaty, as the bushwhacker's horse undoubtedly would have been. All apparently had been waiting for some time.

"What about the stable?" Trevison wondered. "Could do some checking there."

"Doubt if he'd pull into a stable, either. He'd know we'd be looking for his horse and would leave it someplace where we'd not be apt to go — if he stopped in town at all."

"Meaning maybe he kept on going . . ."

"What I'd do if I was him and knew I was being followed."

"Reckon you're right," Boone said, and shifted his attention to the entrance of the Cattleking.

Light was spilling out from above and below the batwing doors, and the lift and fall of voices blending with an occasional thud and the faint tinkle of a piano was a steady sound in the night.

Two riders moved up through the shadows in the street, curved in to the rack, and stopped. Swinging off their saddles, laughing, talking, they tied their mounts alongside the others at the crossbar, stepped up onto the porch and, tramping noisily across its board surface, disappeared into the building. A yell exploded suddenly as friends greeted their arrival.

Shawn glanced toward the center of town. Most of the store windows were black, and there was no one strolling along the sidewalks. He could see a light in the town marshal's office as well as in the lobby of the hotel; otherwise it appeared Carsonville had closed down for the night, leaving all activity to the Cattleking and its one other saloon, the Longhorn.

"Well, we going in?"

At Boone Trevison's question, Shawn nodded. "What we came to town for," he said, and led off, cutting diagonally across the dusty wooden platform and pushing his way through the swinging doors into the wide, smoke-filled room.

The place was crowded, with thirty or forty customers lined up at the bar and gathered at the tables. Two men were behind the counter serving drinks, and a half-dozen women in low-cut, brightly colored dresses that barely reached their knees were moving about joshing with the patrons.

A somewhat older woman sat at the piano, visible through the bluish haze at the rear of the room, patiently laboring at the keys, while two men, leaning against the instrument, were offering an unsteady rendition of the song she was playing.

Starbuck, ignoring the angry looks turned to him as he shouldered his way purposefully through the crowd, drew up at the bar. Creating space for Trevison and himself, he signaled to the round-faced man wearing muttonchops for drinks.

"Whiskey," he ordered, holding up two fingers.

The bartender complied quickly, made change for the double eagle Shawn handed him, and wheeled off in response to another loud request for service.

"You see anybody here from High Green?" Starbuck asked, pivoting slowly about and looking out over the room.

"There in the corner," Boone said, pointing. "There's that jasper we run into this morning — Dixon, I think he said his name was. Them two with him seem familiar, too."

Shawn studied the riders. "They're a couple of the ones that were with him when he stopped us. Wonder how long they've been here."

"Why? You don't figure it was them that —"

"No, but they might've noticed somebody coming in during the last few minutes — besides that pair we saw," Starbuck said, and moving away from the counter, made his way to where Dixon and the other High Green riders were slouched in their chairs. All glanced up as he, with Trevison at his side, halted before them.

Hugh Dixon greeted them with a friendly nod. "See you're already out and around."

"Got to earn our pay," Shawn replied, smiling. "You been here long?"

Dixon frowned, stiffened slightly. "Hell, man, we put in a full day's work. You ain't got no right —"

"Just answer the question," Starbuck said coolly. "I'm not interested in whether you're doing your job or not."

80

Dixon settled back, glanced at his two friends, and shrugged. "Couple of hours, maybe a bit more. Rode in before suppertime — was needing a drink worse'n we needed grub."

"You notice who came in during the last thirty minutes or so?"

Dixon wagged his head. He pointed off in the general direction of the saloon's entrance. "Old Santy Claus hisself could've come through there and we'd a not seen him. Too much smoke and too dang many jaybirds in betwixt us and there."

"You the only High Green hands here tonight?"

"Only ones — leastwise, I ain't seen no others."

"How about Lalicker's bunch?"

"Few of them around, all right. Charlie Vine and them two that sides him — the ones you tangled with — they're here somewheres. Couple others, too, I expect."

Shawn nodded. "Obliged," he said, and turned back into the crowd.

Trevison was directly behind him, and again bulling his way through the press, Shawn crossed to the opposite wall of the room. The piano player had rid herself of the two would-be songbirds, and was now rendering a lively tune that was giving rise to a steady clapping of hands and stomping of feet. Close by, three or four couples were attempting to dance, but with little success.

Halting at a table around which were seated three men, Starbuck pulled back the unused fourth chair and placed it against the wall. He motioned to Trevison.

"You can stand on that," he said.

The gunman favored him with a puzzled look. "Why? What'll I want to get up there for?"

"You're still figuring to speak out, aren't you?" Starbuck asked patiently. "Ought to let everybody in here see who's talking."

Trevison bobbed, immediately stepped up onto the chair. Several persons at adjoining tables paused, glanced at the gunman wonderingly, and then resumed whatever they were doing. The swelling din in the saloon rolled on unabated, and Boone, shaking his head helplessly, started to dismount. Shawn waved him back. Drawing his pistol, he pointed it at the ceiling and fired two quick shots.

The uproar died instantly. Gunsmoke curling about him. Starbuck said, "Man here's got something important to say. Listen."

There was a long hush. Shawn rode it out for several moments, then turned questioningly to Trevison, wondering at the delay. At once the gunman began to speak.

"Name's Boone Trevison. Expect you've already heard of me and why I'm here, but I'll spell it out anyway, in case there's some of you that didn't get the word."

He hesitated. The silence held, an indication to Shawn that people on the Packsaddle had indeed heard of the man and had a healthy respect for him.

"Me and my partner here, Starbuck, have signed on at High Green. Aim to put a stop to all the hell-raising that's been going on there. I'm serving notice right now on all of you here, and everybody else around the country, that we ain't putting up with any more of what's been going on. We've been paid by Aaron Kraft to stop it — and that's sure what we're going to do."

Trevison's voice had grown stronger, harder with each word he spoke. An intensity seemed to fill him, and the fine sweat that gathered on his forehead and cheeks glistened in the smoky light of the big wagon-wheel chandeliers suspended from the ceiling.

"I'm serving notice on everybody: stay off High Green range unless you've got friendly notions! And if there's one more steer slaughtered or blade of grass burned or potshot taken at a Kraft rider, I'll hunt the man down that done it and settle with him personally."

One hand hovering close to the pistol on his hip, the other hooked by a thumb from his cartridge belt, his features hard set, Trevison glared at the crowd as if daring anyone to challenge his words. He waited out several long breaths, and when no one spoke, stepped down from the chair. The silence continued to hold briefly, broke finally as the hubbub of voices began once more.

"That sound all right?" Boone asked anxiously as he faced Starbuck.

"You couldn't have put it better," Shawn replied, starting for the doorway. "Let's get out of here. Place is too crowded to suit me."

"Same here," Trevison muttered, and keeping at Starbuck's heels, followed him through the shifting mass to the batwings and out onto the porch into the cool night air.

"Reckon there won't be no doubt now that we mean business," the gunman said as Shawn moved toward the edge of the porch. "Wasn't nobody wanting to say something back."

"I've got something to say," a voice called from the shadows beyond the flare of light coming from the saloon. "Just you stand where you are and hear me out."

It was John Coon, the town marshal.

CHAPTER
TWELVE

Starbuck drew up, became motionless, his tall figure and that of Boone Trevison distinct in the lamplight.

"Not here, marshal," he said quietly.

Pushing Trevison ahead of him, he stepped down off the porch into a pool of darkness at the edge of the street. Halting there, he moved a step to one side of the gunman where he was able to see the area back of the saloon as well as have an unobstructed view of its entrance. Satisfied, he folded his arms across his chest; he waited for the lawman to speak.

"You, Trevison," Coon said after a time. "Might as well know right now you ain't welcome in my town. I've heard aplenty about you, maybe even got a letter or two about you in my desk. Same probably goes for you, Starbuck."

Shawn's attention was on the saloon, front and rear. The noise within the building had resumed its normal frantic tenor, and activities apparently were again in full sway after the interruption, but there was no real assurance in that; at any moment Charlie Vine or some other man eager to have his try at Boone Trevison could present himself either openly or under cover of the darkness.

85

"You'll find nothing on me, marshal," he said coolly.

Trevison made no comment, evidently finding it unnecessary either to confirm or to deny the possibility. John Coon hawked, spat into the dust.

"Understand this — both of you. I ain't putting up with no foolishness from either of you. Was mighty big talking you done in there —"

"And I aim to back it up," Trevison cut in. "I've been hired to stop all this trouble people around here are giving Aaron Kraft. Exactly what I'll do."

"You start a shooting war, and you'll answer to me!" the lawman shouted angrily.

"I think you've already got one," Starbuck said quietly. "What bothers me is why you haven't done something about it."

"One reason — Aaron Kraft ain't never brought me no proof of who was doing all them things to him."

"You know who it is, same as everybody else does."

"Not talking about that — I'm talking about proof. That's what I've got to have if . . ."

Starbuck's attention settled on the Cattleking's batwings. Three men had emerged, were halting just outside the doors . . . Charlie Vine, Rearick, Bill Bristol . . . Pulling back against the front wall of the saloon, they melted into the shadows on the porch. Drawing his pistol, Shawn came squarely about, faced them.

"You, there," he called sharply. "Either step down here where I can see you, or move on. Don't stand in the dark unless you're looking for trouble."

Coon, interrupted in mid-sentence, and unaware of the Lalicker men's presence, wheeled with a start.

"Who're you talking to?"

"It's only us, marshal," Vine said, and sauntering forward, led his two friends across the porch for the hitchrack. "We was just pulling out."

John Coon, arms at his sides, nodded, wordlessly watched the men mount up and swing back into the street.

"G'night, marshal," Vine said jeeringly as he and the others drifted off into the dark void of the street. "You sleep tight."

Trevison laughed. "Them boys're pretty good friends of yours, I take it."

"No more'n anybody else living around here!" Coon snapped. "And don't you forget it, either! Now, getting back to you and your partner there. I'm going to make this plain as I can: you try taking the law into your own hands, and you'll end up mighty quick inside my jail."

Starbuck shrugged, holstered his gun. "What you're telling us is that we're supposed to stand by, let those night riders go right on killing High Green cattle, burning down line shacks, and doing all those other things, and we're not to do anything to stop it."

Coon spat again. "What I'm saying is, you ain't the law. You come to me when you've got some proof that'll hold up before a judge, then I'll act . . . I ain't about to take a hand in some two-bit squabble between Aaron Kraft and Ford Lalicker."

"Squabble!" Shawn echoed. "From what we've been told, it's gone long past that point — and it's come to where there's going to be some killing over it. You ever ride up to High Green, take a look at the damage that's been done?"

Coon ignored the question, instead seemed to be engrossed in the soaring racket coming from the saloon. Then: "Not saying there ain't been damage and loss. I'm saying there ain't no proof of who done it. Who knows? Maybe it could've been somebody working for Kraft himself — some hired hand with a sticker in his craw."

"You ever try to find out for sure?"

"Nope," the lawman said flatly. "Was always told about it too late. Around here they's a few who don't take much stock in the law — still figure it's up to them personally to look after things same as they did twenty, thirty year ago."

"Could be a reason why," Shawn said.

"Meaning I ain't doing my job?" Coon demanded, bristling.

"Expect you know the answer to that better than I do. Something I've found out knocking around the country is that folks like Aaron Kraft, who've been taking care of their problems for a lot of years, have to be shown before they put much confidence in the law."

"Well, whether they feel that way or not ain't here or there to me. I'm the law, and I aim to keep the peace. Bringing in gunnies like you won't mean nothing but trouble for everybody, and if I can scrape up reason enough, I'll run you both out. Meantime, you best keep your nose clean or —"

"I'll be doing the job I'm getting paid for," Boone Trevison said. "So'll my partner. We expect to look after

88

Mr. Kraft's interests in whatever way's needful. He says Lalicker and some others are after his land."

"Know what he says, and far as I can tell, it could be Kraft's after their places, just like they claim. Ain't no reason why I should believe him quicker'n I would them."

"Except for one thing," Starbuck said. "Nobody's raiding their ranches. All the damage is being done to High Green. That ought to prove something."

"Proves nothing. How do I know Kraft ain't doing things to his place just to make it look bad for Lalicker and the other ranchers around here? And it's a funny thing to me there ain't nobody on Kraft's side at all. Everybody else in the country is standing with Ford Lalicker. Now, that ought to prove something to *you*!"

Starbuck's attention was again on the saloon's doorway. Two men had appeared — strangers who stepped down into the street and hurried off toward the residential area lying east of the settlement. Shawn gave them only scant notice, shifting his gaze instead to a second group that emerged only moments later — Hugh Dixon and the two other riders from High Green.

They did not pause, simply flicked Starbuck and Trevison, and then the lawman, John Coon, with their glances, mounted, and rode out . . . One thing to be said about Aaron Kraft's hired hands, they did nothing more than do the job they were being paid for; there was no common bond uniting them into a single one-for-all-and-all-for-one unit, as was the usual case among ranchhands.

Why? Shawn gave that thought. Was he wrong about Kraft? Was he taking the wrong side in the trouble that was beginning to sweep the Packsaddle country? If so, everything Kraft had told him and Boone Trevison was a lie — just as was all Leda Kraft had said untrue. He found that hard to accept; but, on the other hand, it was difficult to ignore the facts that John Coon had laid out for them.

"Now, I ain't going to stand here all night arguing with you two," Shawn heard the lawman say as Dixon and his friends wheeled off into the darkness. "Far as I'm concerned, bringing you in's only going to make things worse."

"You're forgetting Lalicker make the first move along that line," Starbuck said.

"If you're talking about Charlie Vine and that pair riding with him, no, I ain't forgetting. I told Ford Lalicker he was wrong, and I've give them notice same as I have you."

"You got no call to worry about us," Trevison said. "We ain't going to be hunting for trouble, we'll just be looking to protect Mr. Kraft's property — and we sure got a right to do that."

"Just all depends on how you go about it," Coon said. "Now, like I told you, I ain't warning you again. You maybe're real big with that pistol you're wearing — and I reckon you are, judging from all the tales I've heard told about how fast you are with it and how many men you've killed — but I ain't backing off one inch. Mean everything I've said, and if I have to use a scattergun to make you listen, I'll do it."

90

Abruptly the lawman spun, stalked off down the street in the direction of his quarters.

Trevison, eyes following the old marshal, said, "He's working for Lalicker, can sure see that."

"Possible . . . Could be he's just a man caught in the middle, and way over his head in something he don't know how to handle . . . Let's get to the horses and move out. We're fools to be standing here in the open."

"Thinking that too," Boone said, falling in beside Shawn. "Vine and them two backshooters could be close by somewheres. We don't know for certain they left town, only that we seen them start."

Starbuck nodded, slowed as they came to the rear of the Cattleking.

"Careful," he murmured, raising his hand.

Trevison pulled up short. "What's wrong?"

"Can see a man there with the horses . . . waiting," Shawn replied, drawing his weapon once more. "Let's split — you come in from the right, I'll take the left."

"Mr. Trevison?" a voice called.

Boone paused. "Yeh?"

"Like to talk to you for a minute."

Trevison glanced at Shawn. "Sounds friendly."

Starbuck smiled grimly. "Let's hope," he said quietly. "Go ahead, but keep your eyes peeled. I'll hold my gun on him . . . Could be a trap."

CHAPTER
THIRTEEN

Crouched in the darkness at the back of the saloon, Starbuck watched Boone Trevison cross in short, firm steps to the hitchrack. Although the moon was out and the country was flooded with its glowing silver light, the buildings, trees, and brush clumps laid patches of deep shadows here and there. It was in one such area that the man who had called to Trevison was waiting; thus he was not clearly visible.

Attention riveted to the stranger, Shawn continued to maintain his vigilance. It could be one of Aaron Kraft's hired hands, he thought — but that seemed unlikely. It was only logical to believe a High Green rider would have made his presence known earlier inside the saloon if he had something to say; too, it was equally reasonable to think he would have been with Hugh Dixon and the other Kraft men.

Shawn reckoned he could remove Dixon and the two who'd been with him in the Cattleking off the list of possible traitors working for the rancher. Their horses had been at the hitchrack at the edge of the street, and none of the animals had been ridden for several hours — solid proof that none of them could have been the bushwhacker. But they were only a small part of Aaron Kraft's crew.

Lige Hathaway — High Green's foreman — his brother, Joe, and the rider that had been dispatched to warn others on the ranch, Dan Chesser, all knew about the visit he and Trevison were planning to make in town that night. So would all the others Chesser had passed the word to.

Eyes still on the vague figures of Trevison and the stranger, now in conversation, Starbuck listened idly to the muted thump of feet to music, the rumble of voices and other sounds seeping through the thin walls of the saloon. Dixon and his two companions were the only ones he could eliminate from his list of suspects, he guessed; and the number that remained was so large that he might as well forget trying to figure out just who the guilty man was, at least until something developed that would narrow down possibilities.

Dropping back a step, Shawn had a long look at the end of the street and the land beyond into which Vine, Al Rearick, and Bill Bristol had disappeared. There was no sign of anyone, and returning again to his place against the wall, he once more gave the area lying behind the saloon a careful probing. Only Trevison and the man who had called to him were to be seen — and they no more than indefinite blurs near the horses.

He wished Boone and whoever the stranger was would have done with whatever they were discussing. He didn't like the idea of the gunman exposing himself as he was doing. They would both be much better off in the saddle and on their way through the forested slopes, en route to High Green. If any attempt . . .

Starbuck grunted in satisfaction. The stranger had suddenly turned, was hurrying off into the alley that lay behind the store buildings on that side of the street. Still cautious, however, Shawn crossed to where Trevison was pulling free the bay's reins and was preparing to mount.

Holstering his pistol, Shawn unwound his own leathers and went onto the saddle. "What was that all about?"

"Was doing me a favor — tipping me off about a raid," Boone answered as they swung away from the rack.

"Raid? On Kraft's place?"

"Yeh. Going to be a bunch hit some stock Aaron's got grazing down on his lower range about daybreak tomorrow. Wanted to let me know, so's I could be there waiting."

Starbuck, avoiding the street and keeping to the darker areas as they moved on for the road to High Green, gave that thought.

"Plenty nice of him," he said doubtfully. "Why did he do it? Everybody's said to be against Kraft."

"Doing it for me, not Aaron Kraft," Trevison said, pride in his voice. "Reckon it's to be expected after me laying down that warning back there in the saloon. Be a lot of men right anxious to become my friends now."

"That the reason he gave?"

"More or less. Called me Mr. Trevison so many times that I —"

94

"Who was he?" Shawn wondered, his skepticism mounting steadily.

"Didn't want to give me his name. Said it would be worth his life if it ever got around that he'd warned me."

"He somebody you've seen before?"

"Don't think so. Sort of kept his face turned away from me so's I couldn't get a good look at him, I guess ... Can't blame him. If any of them Lalicker hands knew he'd talked to me ..."

"Could be they do," Starbuck said.

They had reached the fork in the road north of the settlement and were turning onto the branch that led to the mountains. At once Shawn veered away from the open, well-marked trail and cut off into the brush along its shoulders. Their passage would be less noticeable, and they would not offer easy targets for another bushwhacker, should one be lying in wait somewhere on ahead.

"What's that mean?" Trevison asked in a rising voice. He seemed unaware of the precaution Starbuck had taken.

"Could be a trick. Lalicker or maybe Charlie Vine sent him to tell you that — and it'll be them waiting for you instead of the other way around."

Boone swore. "Hell, I don't figure it as that way. Man was honest ..."

"How do you know? You never saw him before. He wouldn't tell you his name, and he wouldn't let you get a good look at him."

"Told you why he was so careful, and far as I'm concerned, his reasons make sense. Actually, the man was sort a scared of me — wanted to do me a favor and show me he was on my side. Could say it was out of respect."

Shawn, eyes roving the shadowy country around them as he continually searched out the dark, smiled faintly. "Possible . . . Guess I'm a bit short on faith in people, however."

Trevison remained silent as they rode steadily on, climbing gradually into the higher levels of the hills. They were well off the road, moving along the aisles between the pines and other trees, with Starbuck a length ahead of the gunman, choosing a path that avoided the open, moonlit areas. The night was warm and pleasant, and from far down on the slope below them a mockingbird was filling the night with his song.

"I'm wondering if whoever it was that sent you that message didn't have something else in mind."

Boone shrugged, spat. "Ain't saying you're right in what you're thinking . . . but figuring you are — what do you mean?"

"It could be a move to draw us and the High Green crew down to one end of Kraft's range. That would leave the other end wide open for Lalicker's bunch to do what they pleased."

Trevison pulled off his hat, ran splayed fingers through his hair. "Just can't make myself believe that man was cold-decking me! Somehow I get the feeling he was on the level and was really wanting to do me a favor."

96

"He say where he got the information?"

"Claimed he overheard some of Lalicker's hired help talking in the Longhorn saloon. He was standing at the bar, he said, and they was playing cards at a table right behind him. They didn't catch on that he was listening."

Starbuck frowned. "If he was at the Longhorn, how'd he know about you being at the Cattleking?"

"Never asked. Expect he left there and come up to where we was. Come in in time to hear me laying down the law, anyway. Did mention that."

"He say when — about what time, I mean — that he heard them talking?"

"No, reckon it was early this evening — not that it'd make any difference just when. Could've been most anytime today."

"Not quite. Hardly anybody knew we'd gone to work for Kraft until we rode back to town late this afternoon — or even knew who you were until you made that speech, far as that goes."

"You're forgetting Charlie Vine and them others. They seen us when we first rode in. But what the hell! I reckon we could keep jawing this around to where it'd get so mixed up we never would get it flattened out to our liking . . . Anyways, I'm going to believe what he told me, put it down in my hat as a favor."

"Which means you're taking him at his word."

"Yes, sir. Way I look at it, there's just as good a chance he was telling me the truth as he was doing what you think — setting me up for an ambush or fixing it so's they could do a lot of hell-raising on Kraft's range."

Boone Trevison was a trusting soul, Shawn concluded as they rode on, but undoubtedly he knew what he was doing, otherwise he would not have lived to be there sitting astride his bay horse and talking about what was to come, or have earned the reputation he owned. Perhaps the fault lay with himself, Starbuck thought; maybe he had allowed too many disappointments and failures to dampen his trust in other men.

"All up to you," he said, surrendering. "You're calling the shots, and whatever you figure's the thing to do, you can count on me backing you all the way."

"Glad to hear that, Shawn. We get back to the ranch, I'll hunt up that foreman, Hathaway, tell him I want a half-dozen good men to ride with us in the morning. Like to be setting there waiting when that bunch from Lalicker's shows up. They'll sure be surprised to find us all cocked and primed for them."

Starbuck raised his glance. They were almost to the hogback. The ranch lay only minutes beyond.

"Still a while short of midnight. Could hold off a few hours before you talk to Hathaway. He'll be sleeping . . . and I reckon we could both use a little ourselves."

"Yeh, for a fact," Trevison said, and yawned. "Have to get down on that lower range where they're aiming to pull off that raid plenty early, however. Important thing is to be there when they show up."

If they show up, Starbuck thought. In spite of his declaration to Boone that he would go along with his plan, Shawn was becoming more convinced that it was all a ruse to catch High Green off guard, inflict serious damage on one area of Kraft's range while the crew, led by the man hired to protect and halt such depredations, was somewhere in the opposite direction waiting for raiders who would never appear.

But there was no use talking to Trevison about it. The gunman had made up his mind to believe the warning given him by the stranger, and would hear of nothing else. Shawn would have to take it on his own shoulders, he realized, to see that High Green was not left unprotected — and he would have to do it in such a way that Boone Trevison would not feel his authority was being disputed and his wishes ignored.

Just how he could manage that, Starbuck was not certain, but it had to be done — and he didn't have many hours in which to come up with an answer.

CHAPTER
FOURTEEN

"Something's wrong," Trevison said as they topped out the rocky ridge and dropped over into the broad valley in which lay High Green.

Starbuck had to agree. The ranch, which could be expected to be in darkness at that late hour, was ablaze with light.

"Let's get down there," Shawn murmured, and raking the sorrel with his spurs, sent the big gelding loping through the night.

They came into the yard minutes later, to find Lige Hathaway and several other members of the crew gathered in front of the cook shack, nursing cups of black coffee and smoking nervously. Aaron Kraft and Leda were up also, and as Shawn and Trevison swung into the yard and halted at a hitchrack, both came out of the main house onto the porch and paused on the steps.

"Was getting plumb worried about you," Hathaway said, watching Starbuck and the gunman dismount. "Fact is, we was just about to mount up a posse and go looking for you."

Shawn heaved a sigh. There had been no trouble at the ranch, as he had first feared; it was simply that their delay in returning had given rise to the belief that something had gone wrong.

"Dixon told us what happened there in the saloon, how Trevison there got up and told the whole danged town how the cow ate the cabbage, far as High Green's concerned."

Boone nodded, grinned happily, and glanced toward Kraft and the girl. Starbuck said, "He tell you about the marshal jumping us . . . and Charlie Vine and his friends hanging around for a bit, too?"

"Nope, never mentioned that."

"Would've helped if Dixon and the men with him had stood up, made a show of backing us."

"Hugh and them just never thought, I reckon. Been sort of the trouble here on High Green — ain't never no spirit like there ought to be. Boys just do their job and not give a goddamn about nothing else. Working, eating, sleeping, and drawing wages, that's all it amounts to."

The foreman paused, cocked his head to one side. "Got me a hunch Trevison's changed that some," he continued. "He's sort of built a fire under everybody with that talking he done, made them proud to be working for High Green."

"What I was hoping to do," Trevison said. "Only way we can come out on top is for us all to be pulling together."

"That's for sure," one of the men muttered. "Been the other way around — mostly."

"Ain't saying the boys was doing anything a'purpose," Hathaway added. "Just weren't nobody heading up things."

101

"What're we doing next?" another rider asked in an eager voice. "We taking a little sashay over to Lalicker's place, let them know we — ?"

"No," Starbuck cut in before Boone could give an answer. "Need to avoid that kind of a run-in unless we're crowded."

"Seems to me that's done happened. They been dealing us hell, and we ain't hardly been doing anything to pay them back. I figure we ought —"

"Just hold on, Andy," Hathaway cut in. "Best we leave this kind of business up to Trevison, not be trying to tell him what he ought to do. It's him that's got the know-how when it comes to handling trouble."

"That's a good idea," Starbuck said, and turning to the gunman, basking in the admiring attention of the riders, pointed toward the main house. "Looks like the boss is waiting to have a word with you."

Trevison shifted his glance to Kraft and his daughter. "Expect they do," he said briskly. "You think you can get things set up for me in the morning?"

"Can leave it all up to me," Shawn replied. "You go ahead."

Boone started to turn, move off across the hardpack. He slowed his steps, looked back at Hathaway and the others. "Starbuck there knows what I want done. You listen to him, do whatever he says. Be the same as taking orders from me."

Shawn watched the gunman continue on for the house, well pleased. This solved the problem that was troubling him: he could go ahead and handle matters in the way he thought best. Coming back around, he faced the High Green foreman and the short dozen riders with him.

"Want you all to go crawl into your bunks. I know Trevison appreciates how you feel about him and what he's done, but you're going to need some sleep, and now's the time to get it. Like as not you won't have much chance in the next few days . . . Lige, there's some things we need to talk over — some planning to do."

Hathaway nodded, pointed to the cabin, once his, now occupied by Shawn and the gunman.

"Can go in there if it's private."

"It is," Starbuck said, and started across the yard for the small structure standing at its south edge.

The Krafts, with Boone, had reentered the main house. Shawn could see them seated about a table in the kitchen. Leda was pouring coffee, and it appeared she intended serving something else — pie, most likely. Off in the direction of the bunkhouse he could hear the shuffling sound of the crew as they headed for their quarters.

"First off," Starbuck said as he pushed open the cabin door, "somebody tried bushwhacking Trevison and me when we rode into town."

"Bushwacked!" Hathaway echoed, waiting while Shawn struck a match to a lamp sitting on the table. "He hit one of you?"

"Trevison got a scratch. We were both lucky, I reckon. Point that's bothering me is this: I figure it was somebody working for you. Means we've got a traitor on Kraft's payroll."

The foreman was silent for a time. Finally he wagged his head, settled down onto one of the straight-backed chairs.

"That's sure kind of hard to believe, but I ain't saying it's not possible. You got any idea who it is?"

"Not yet. Thought maybe you would."

"Nope, sure ain't. Most of the hands've been here for quite a spell. Chesser's kind of new . . . and so's Andy Pogue."

"Chesser — he's the one you sent out to tell the rest of the crew about Trevison and me being on the job."

"Yeh, you recollect him — he was standing there handy like in the doorway of the bunkhouse. You think maybe he's the one?"

"Could be, but it easy could be somebody else, maybe one of the men he told about Boone and me and that had time to ride down and be waiting along the road."

"Can see that . . . and that covers a dozen or more who were working close enough to do that. You got something in mind you want done about it?"

"Just keep it under your hat, but do some watching and listening. Need to figure out who it was and nail him before he can do us any damage . . . Now, about tomorrow morning."

Hathaway looked up. "What about tomorrow morning?"

Starbuck told the foreman of Trevison's talk with the stranger in the darkness behind the Cattleking saloon and of the raid that was to take place on High Green's south range.

104

"Trevison wants to be there ready and waiting," Shawn explained. "Like to have three or four men ride with us — leave early enough to be there by first light."

"They're figuring on hitting what we call the Meadows . . . Means you'll need to leave here around four o'clock. You know who this bird was that warned Trevison?"

"No, was careful to hide his face from Boone, and he wouldn't tell his name. What's down there on that part of the range, anything special?"

"Nothing more'n usual — fifteen or sixteen hundred cows grazing."

"How many riders have you got looking after them?"

"Three, maybe four . . ."

Starbuck nodded. "Can use them if it turns out there was something to the warning."

Hathaway scratched at the whiskers on his jaw. "You don't figure there is?"

"Just not taking it for gospel," Starbuck said, shrugging. "Was all too easy, too pat. I mentioned that to Trevison, but he can't see it that way. He's sure the fellow was telling the truth — and maybe he was. I could be a mite too suspicious."

"But you ain't willing to let it go at that. Can see you're thinking something else."

"Ruling out that it's not a raid on Kraft's herd, or a trap for Trevison, but only a trick to get us all down at that part of the range, what's up at the other end that they could hit — something that would really hurt Kraft?"

Hathaway's jaw sagged. "Hell, that special breeding stock Aaron's fooling around with's up there! Got it penned up in Box Canyon, place close to Clancy's Peak. That's about as far north as you can get on High Green range."

"Which puts it near Lalicker's . . ."

"On west a piece, but not far. When Aaron got it in his head to try breeding up his stock, we looked around for a place closer to here so's we could watch it better. Just wasn't nothing suitable, so we had to settle for Box Canyon. It's got good water, plenty of grass, and was easy to shut off so's the other stock couldn't go mixing in."

"Would Lalicker know about it?"

"Everybody in the country knows about it! Aaron brought that bull in all the way from Nebraska. Paid a bushel of cash for him, and —"

"I'll lay odds that's where the raid will be if there's one coming," Starbuck broke in. "Means we'll have to cover both places — Box Canyon and the Meadows."

"That's for certain. You want me to take a few of the boys and sentry the canyon?"

Shawn nodded. "Pick ones you know can be trusted, and however many you think will be enough. Have them scattered and in place by first light. May all be for nothing, but we'd best not take any chance."

"You and Trevison'll look after the Meadows?"

"Yes. He's sold on the idea that's where the trouble will be, and maybe he's right. But this way, covering both ends, we won't get caught with our britches down."

106

Starbuck got to his feet, looked through the open doorway toward the house. Boone was still at the table with Leda Kraft and her father. The girl faced the yard, and he could see that she was smiling, apparently having warmed up considerably to Boone since his exploits in the Cattleking.

"Reckon I'd best be getting along, grabbing myself a mite of shut-eye," Hathaway said, rising. "Pulling out at 4a.m. means climbing out of bed some earlier so's to be on time. I'll drop by, do some talking to Hobie, tell him to have a pot of coffee ready."

"Good idea," Starbuck said as the foreman stepped out into the yard. "One more thing . . ."

"Yeh?"

"The men you're sending with Trevison and me — I'd like for one of them to be Dan Chesser."

"Chesser? I thought you sort of —"

"If he's along with me, I can watch him easier. Good night . . ."

"G'night," Hathaway replied, and continued on his way.

CHAPTER
FIFTEEN

The air was sharp, biting. Starbuck drew his bush jacket tighter about his torso, fastened the top button as he rode out of the yard that next morning well before daylight. To his left, muttering at the cold and wearing a borrowed windbreaker, was Boone Trevison, while on the opposite side of the sorrel were the two men delegated to accompany them to the Meadows — Dan Chesser and a rider about his own age who said his name was Tom Orr.

Trevison had made no comment when he learned that Shawn was sending a party to the upper end of High Green's range as a precaution, seemed more interested in the fact that he had spent well over an hour in the company of Aaron and Leda Kraft that previous evening, during which they had made it clear they were more than pleased with him and what he had done in the Cattleking.

"Aaron's hinting about me sticking around once I've got this here mess with Lalicker cleaned up," he said as they rode steadily on through the half-dark.

"Partnership?"

"Ain't exactly sure what he means. Kind of got the idea, though, that he was sort of hoping me and his daughter'd get together . . . She was plenty nice there last night. Real friendly, and kept feeding me pie and coffee till I like to bust."

"Leda's a fine girl," Shawn said. "You sure couldn't do much better than winding up being Aaron Kraft's son-in-law."

Trevison laughed, made an offhand gesture. "Well, it ain't gone that far yet, of course, but I kind of think it's heading that way."

Starbuck turned his attention to Dan Chesser. The rider had not been particularly happy at being chosen to be a member of the party, but Lige Hathaway had taken no back talk from him. He rode now, shoulders slumped, chin deep in his chest, eyes straight ahead as they moved through the trees fringing the grassy flat en route to the Meadows.

Orr, however, had been more than happy at his selection. That he considered it a privilege to be riding with Boone Trevison was evident, and shortly he dropped back from his position beside Chesser, and circling, eased up to where he was next to the gunman. They fell into immediate conversation, with Orr asking Boone many questions about his experiences and such — all of which Trevison answered with obvious relish.

Starbuck, glad to have the gunman otherwise occupied, kneed his sorrel in nearer to Chesser. "You able to get around to all the crew yesterday?"

Chesser looked up, nodded woodenly. "Just about."

"Big ranch. Can see where it'd take time."

Dan had lapsed again into a sullen silence.

"Figured to see you in town last night," Shawn continued. "Got the notion somehow you were riding in."

Chesser stirred once more. "Why, was you looking for me?"

"Sort of. Ran into Hugh Dixon and a couple other boys. Expected you'd be with them."

"Ain't the ones I run with. Besides, I usually do my drinking at the Longhorn."

"Explains why I missed you. We were at the Cattleking . . . They hear about Trevison down there?"

"Yeh, somebody come in telling about it."

"Somebody from Lalicker's?"

Chesser drew up slowly, shifted on his saddle. He was quiet for a long breath and then shrugged. "Don't rightly recollect who it was."

Starbuck grinned. "Well, no matter. Important thing is that everybody knows about it now."

"Yeh, reckon they do."

Shawn turned to the land around them. The swale along which they were riding extended on indefinitely, floored by a soft-appearing carpet of grass that looked silver in the light of the stars and lowering moon rather than green. Small, mirrorlike water holes were visible on occasion, and the tall pines rimming the lush area were as dark-clad soldiers standing rigidly at attention. If all of Aaron Kraft's forty thousand acres were similar to this, he was indeed a wealthy man.

A small spot of red loomed in the distance. Tom Orr said, "That'll be the camp. We can cut straight across and save —"

110

"Stay in the trees," Starbuck said quickly. "Want to keep from being seen . . . Where'll the herd be?"

"Probably somewheres east of them. Heard Lige telling some of the boys to drift the stock off in that direction a few days back."

"We'll come in from the side and pull up in the trees. Can keep from ever showing ourselves that way."

"Got to let them boys at the camp know we're here . . . and why," Trevison said. "We'll be needing their guns if things happen like I figure they will."

"Aimed to have Tom ride over, once we get set, tell them what's going on. Anybody watching will think he's one of the nighthawks coming in to the fire for a cup of coffee."

"Yeh, that ought to fool them. Where you reckon Lalicker's bunch'll come in from?"

"Chesser or Tom can probably answer that, they both knowing the country."

"From the south," Orr said at once. "Easier to reach the Meadows. Country's a mite rough, on due east. Horse running hard in the dark could break a leg. Ain't that what you think, Dan?"

Chesser mumbled his agreement.

"Then we'd best circle around, get set on that far side," Boone said. "That'll be below the herd, if I'm understanding you right."

"Yes, sir," the younger man said. "You want me to wait till you've got clean around before I go tell the boys, or is it all right if I do it now?"

"Go ahead," Trevison said with a wave of his hand. "Can't see as it'll make any difference."

Temper flared through Starbuck. "Does make a difference!" he snapped. "Want those cowhands to know exactly where we'll be hiding . . . and Tom won't know himself until he sees where we stop. I'm not anxious to get myself or any of you shot accidentally, and we'll be in a crossfire if Lalicker's bunch comes in from below us like we figure they will."

"That's right," Boone said agreeably. "Better hold off, Tom, until we get located."

Starbuck settled back, satisfied, his anger cooling as suddenly as it had surfaced. One thing he could say about the gunman, he was willing to concede when he was wrong.

A half-hour later they had circled the herd and were pulling into a cluster of trees and brush jutting out from a larger grove along the lower edge of the pasture-like area. The need to make their presence known to the High Green riders at the camp became unnecessary shortly after their arrival, when they came up on one of the nighthawks, a man Tom Orr called Avery. He was given complete details by Trevison of the anticipated raid and told what was to be done once trouble started, instructions he immediately carried on to the camp, since light was already beginning to brighten the eastern sky.

"Stay in the saddle," Boone directed after Avery had ridden on. "Got to be ready to move fast."

"We just let them come in, that it?" Orr asked.

The gunman nodded. "Figure to work it like a trap. We set quiet, let them ride on by, then we'll swing in

112

behind them. The rest of the men'll come at them from the front, squeeze them in between us."

Starbuck glanced again to the east. The pale flare was spreading rapidly. If the man who had warned Boone was telling the truth, the raiders would be showing up at any moment.

Time dragged by. Minutes became a half-hour. The grassy land before them, thickly sprinkled with cattle, was now in full daylight. Over beyond the herd, the men of the night crew were mounting up, drifting restlessly back and forth, uncertain if they should continue standing by or go about their usual duties.

"They ain't coming," Trevison said finally, putting words to the thoughts in all their minds. "Something's happened. My guess is that word leaked out and they knew we'd be waiting, so they called it off."

That was possible, Starbuck realized, but there was one thing they could be certain of; it could not have been Dan Chesser who had warned Lalicker. The rider hadn't been out of his sight since being told of the plan.

"Beginning to look that way," he said, answering Trevison.

He hoped that such was the fact, for if not, and it had all been a ruse designed to leave the upper end of High Green unprotected, then Lige Hathaway and the men he'd taken with him to Box Canyon were probably at that very moment making a stand.

"Let's give it till sunrise. If they haven't come by then, we'll head back to the ranch."

"Not much use waiting," Trevison said. He was showing no disappointment, only a sort of weary acceptance. "They'd've been here by now if they was coming . . . Could do this, sort of play it safe and leave Tom and Chesser with the crew, so's there'll be plenty of help around."

Shawn nodded. He would as soon keep Dan Chesser within sight, but it seemed to him it had gotten to where he continually opposed Boone, and he reckoned it didn't really matter, anyway; let the two men stay.

"Suits me," he said, and wheeling the sorrel about, started diagonally across the swale to pick up the trail on its yonder side. He heard Boone set forth more instructions to young Tom Orr and Chesser, and then shortly the gunman caught up and was at his side.

"Lalicker's bunch got tipped off, sure's hell," Trevison said. "Only explanation. Somebody told them we'd be waiting, and they backed off, scared to try whatever it was they was aiming to do."

"Can't blame them for not wanting to ride into a trap."

"Sure can't, but it's mighty disappointing. Was hoping we could have it out with them."

Starbuck had no comment for that, and they rode on in silence, now keeping to the open range, where the horses had easier going. A time later they climbed out of the low, sweeping hollow, crossed a flat, and crowning a rise, looked down on the ranch.

Shawn frowned, his attention sharpening. Several men were gathered in the yard at the back of the house. It was too far to recognize any of those present other than the squat figure of Aaron Kraft.

"Looks like there's been trouble," he said, and put the sorrel into a hard gallop. Trevison immediately spurred his horse into a like gait.

They came into the yard together, drew up near the waiting men, who turned to face them. Trevison was off the saddle first. He hurried to Kraft.

"What's going on?"

The rancher wagged his head dolefully. "All hell busted loose up at Box Canyon, where I got some special breeding stock. Them damned raiders tried to get to them. Lige Hathaway and a half-dozen of the boys stopped them from doing anything."

"Good!" Trevison said. "Sure glad he was there watching out for us."

"I reckon Lige ain't so happy about it," one of the riders said dryly. "He went and got hisself killed."

CHAPTER
SIXTEEN

"Lige Hathaway . . . dead?" Trevison said in a disbelieving voice.

"Sure is," the rider replied. "His brother, Joe, and the rest of the party'll be here in a bit. They're bringing in the body. I come on ahead."

"Anybody else hurt?" Starbuck asked.

"Yeh, couple of the boys got shot up some."

There was no doubt now; it had been a trick, one calculated to draw off High Green's crew, have them at the far end of the range so that the raiders could have a free hand in Box Canyon, where Kraft had his prize cattle.

Trevison turned to Starbuck. His face was stern. "How many men did you send with Lige?"

"Left it up to him . . ."

"Was four of us, and Lige," the rider said. "Couple others joined us when we got to the canyon. Made seven, all told . . . Was a dozen or more of the Lalicker outift."

"You for certain that's who it was?"

"Why, hell yes! Who else could it've been? They just rode in, not figuring anybody was around, so I got a good look at them. Spotted three or four that I know works for Lalicker. And then, that Charlie Vine, and that pair that side him all the time, was there."

"You see Lalicker himself?"

"Ain't sure, but I think he was with them, sort of hanging back, watching."

Boone Trevison again put his attention on Starbuck. "Expect you should've seen to it that Hathaway took along more help. Damn shame let a man like him get killed."

Impatience ripped through Shawn. An angry retort formed on his lips, but Aaron Kraft spoke before he could make his answer.

"Lige was doing what he was paid to do," the rancher said. "Hate what's happened, but he knew what he was up against . . . and he was a growed man. No sense blaming anybody but Ford Lalicker for him being dead . . . I take it you didn't run into no trouble at the Meadows?"

Trevison said, "Nobody showed up. I figure they got tipped off that we'd be waiting for them."

"Be my guess they never aimed to," Kraft said, shrugging. "Was all just a stunt to get you and my crew out of the way. Lucky you thought to send Lige and some of the boys up to Box Canyon. It's bad the way it turned out for him, but they did keep that thieving bunch from doing a lot of damage. I got a lot of time and money invested in the stock penned up in there."

"Just trying to keep all the gates closed," Boone said grandly. "It's what you're paying me for, and I believe in giving a man a day's work for a day's wages." The gunman paused, slid a covert glance at Starbuck, and

117

then continued. "You know, I had a hunch getting me down to your south range was only a trick. Reason why I wanted Box Canyon protected. I was only . . ."

Shawn, a half-smile tugging at his lips, turned away as the sound of horses coming into the yard reached him. Boone Trevison had been scarcely aware of men being sent to watch over Aaron Kraft's prized breeding stock, but if he wanted to take credit for it, let him. That was neither here nor there. The important, and sad, thing about it was that a good man had been killed and others hurt doing the job . . . And it could signal the opening of a bloody war.

"Here's Joe and the boys now," the rider who had come in ahead with the bad news said.

Joe Hathaway, trailing a horse over which the body of his brother had been hung, was leading the party. Next were two men sitting slumped on their saddles. Blood stained the shirt of one, the pants leg of the other.

At that moment Leda Kraft came out onto the porch and down into the yard. "Have those wounded men come into the house so's I can tend them," she ordered in a businesslike voice.

"Maybe best to send them on to town, let Doc Eiseman fix them up," Kraft said.

"Need some attention first," the girl replied. "Could bleed to death riding that far."

Kraft nodded, beckoned to the wounded men, and pointed at the house. "My daughter'll look after you."

Joe Hathaway had pulled to a stop in the center of the yard. More of High Green's crew were coming up,

118

and a fair-sized crowd was gathering around him. All were tight-lipped, angry.

"Lige's dead," Hathaway said, "but I reckon Harmon's already told you that. Was the Lalickers that done it."

"Any of them get shot?" Kraft asked.

"We winged a couple of them," one of the other members of the party said. "Don't know how bad, but they was pulling leather when we drove them off."

"What we do know is it was all Ford Lalicker's doing," Hathaway said grimly. "And he's going to pay for killing my brother!"

A rumble of agreement ran through the crowd. Someone said, "I'm for paying them back good this time! No more of this pussyfooting — Lalicker's ought to be burned to the ground!"

"And he ain't the only one," another rider shouted, making himself heard. "There's them that's lined up with Lalicker — Bradley and McCroden and Wescott, a couple others. They was in on the killing as much as Lalicker, and the way I see it, they all got something coming to them."

"I'm betting some of that bunch was from their ranches! I'm betting they wasn't all Lalicker's crew."

Kraft raised his hands, palms spread, to command silence. When the jumble of voices had ceased, he turned to Hathaway. "What about it, Joe? You spot anybody from McCroden's and the other ranches?"

The younger Hathaway stirred wearily. "I just don't recollect. It all happened real sudden like. We was in two bunches, one on each side of the canyon right outside the mouth. Wasn't nothing going on, and then, the next thing I knew, they was riding up to the gate in the fence like they owned the place.

"Lige stood up and yelled for them to turn around, get the hell out of there. He'd hardly got it out of his mouth when they opened up. Lige got hit first off. He sort of fell on me, and I was looking after him while the boys was shooting back. Got in a few shots, howsomever. Could see Lige was dead, so I grabbed up my gun and started pulling the trigger fast as I could. The Lalicker crowd was leaving by then, but I'm pretty sure I got me one of them. Seen him sort of flinch."

"Well, you'll be getting another chance at them, Joe," the man called Harmon said. "We're ready to ride with you, soon's you're ready . . . What about Lige?"

Hathaway glanced at his brother, then to Kraft. "Sort of like to bury him here on the ranch, if it's all right with you. High Green's the closest thing to a home he's ever had, 'cepting for the place where we was born."

Kraft said, "Sure. Here's the right place for him. I'll have somebody nail a coffin together."

"Be obliged to you, and I'm hoping you'll say a few words over him."

"If that's what you want. Might be better was I to send for the preacher . . ."

"No, I'd rather you'd do it. Lige never did put much stock in preachers and churches and such, only in his friends — and he figured you for one of his best. I know he'd want you to be doing it."

"Then that's how it'll be."

120

"Obliged . . . I'd sort of like to get it done right away."

"All right, but it'll take a couple of hours to knock the coffin together and get the grave dug."

"That'll be fine. Still early, so there'll be plenty of time for us to be paying that visit to Lalicker's and the others' places once Lige is in the ground."

"Might be smart to wait till dark," someone suggested.

"The smartest thing you can do is forget it," Starbuck, silent up to that moment, cut in. "You can't go at it that way, Joe. What you're planning means a lot more killing."

A shout of protest went up from the crew. Harmon said, "They got it coming to them!"

"Maybe so, but some of you'll likely end up dead too — best you think of that before you go off halfcocked. They'll be expecting you, after what's happened. You won't catch them off guard."

"Won't matter," Boone Trevison said, moving up to Hathaway's side. "We can take care of them. They've started a shooting war, I figure it's up to us to finish it."

Shawn turned to the gunman. "Maybe you like to see dead men — I don't. I think we'd best handle this through the law." He paused, faced Kraft. "That what you think?"

The rancher looked startled. He frowned, rubbed at his jaw, finally bobbed his head. "Yeh, expect that's what we ought to do first — go see John Coon."

"He ain't never been no help before!" one of the riders protested.

"Maybe he hasn't had anything he could work from before," Starbuck said evenly. "A man's been killed now, and that changes everything."

"What's that mean?" Joe Hathaway wondered.

"That you ought to leave it up to Mr. Kraft, Trevison, and me. You go ahead, get ready to bury your brother. Could have the funeral at sundown. Meantime, we'll ride in to town, have a talk with the marshal."

Trevison, quick to sense the change in the rancher's attitude, nodded. "That's the right way to do it. Then, if the law won't take a hand, we'll just do the job ourselves."

Joe Hathaway glanced about at the crew uncertainly, some muttering their opposition, others agreeing. Hugh Dixon stepped up, laid a hand on his knee.

"Won't hurt none to let them try. And you oughtn't to rush the burying. Sundown'll be a fine time to put Lige away."

Hathaway gave that a few moments' thought, stirred on his saddle. "All right, I can't see as it'll make any difference. You all go see the marshal," he said, and putting his horse into motion, moved off toward the bunkhouse.

CHAPTER
SEVENTEEN

"Expect this here's a waste of time," Aaron Kraft said, brushing at the sweat beads gathered on his florid face.

Starbuck gave no thought to the rancher's comment, his eyes instead on several horses standing in front of Marshal John Coon's office at the far end of the street. With Kraft and Boone Trevison, he had mounted immediately after talking Joe Hathaway into delaying any attempt at reprisal until the lawman could be made aware of the situation, and ridden to the settlement.

"Goes for what I'm thinking, too," the gunman declared. "Whatever's done, we'll have to do ourselves. Far as I'm concerned, it would've been better if I'd taken a bunch of the boys and paid a call on Lalicker."

"You'd not found him at home," Kraft said, his attention now with Starbuck's on the marshal's office. "If I ain't wrong, he's there visiting John Coon right now — along with some of his friends."

Shawn murmured in satisfaction. "Couldn't be much better."

"You mean having a showdown with him?" Boone asked.

"No, we can now charge him with the death of Lige Hathaway, or leastwise for causing it, right to his face."

"Talking's not my idea of settling things," the gunman said in a rough voice. "Only thing a jasper like him savvies is a gun. You say the word, Aaron, and I'll get this business with him fixed up once and for good before we leave town."

Shawn threw an angry glance at the rancher. "If that's how you want it, count me out, beginning right now! I'm not —"

"We'll try it your way first, Starbuck," Kraft said quietly. "I'm a reasonable man, but I'm tired of the way things've been going. I want to get this settled, one way or another. I'm full up to my gullet of Ford Lalicker and them tail-kissers running with him."

"You just leave it all to me," Trevison said briskly as they angled into the jail's hitchrack. "If you don't get no sense out of that marshal, then I'll take over."

Starbuck, at last weary of the gunman's persistent aggressiveness, turned to him impatiently. "Goddamnit! Can't you forget about that pistol you're packing? There's ways of straightening out things besides spilling blood!"

Boone, suddenly stiff with anger, swung off his horse. "And maybe you're forgetting who's running this show, mister," he said coldly. "I —"

"Never mind," Kraft broke in sharply. "We'll do some talking first. Plenty of time for using a gun later, if need be."

Starbuck, dismounting, temper cooling, stepped up onto the small square of wooden landing fronting the building. His eyes were on the men inside Coon's office. There were four besides the lawman himself.

124

"Is one of them Lalicker?" he asked.

Kraft paused at his shoulder. "Yeh, tall one with the sharp face, sandy moustache. That's McCroden with the knife scar on his chin. Young one in the black hat's Dave Wescott. Carl Mayberry's the other'n . . . Sure like to know what they're doing here and just what they're telling John Coon."

"Only one way to find out," Starbuck said, and led the way into the marshal's quarters.

The ranchers, hearing the beat of boot heels on the board platform, had all turned, were watching them as they entered. With the exception of Lalicker, in whose eyes there was the glow of pure hate, their features were expressionless.

Coon, standing behind his desk, let his gaze rest briefly on Kraft, then shifted it to Starbuck and to Trevison.

"Now, there'll be no trouble here," he began in a taut voice. "If you aim —"

"We're here to swear out a complaint," Starbuck said when no words came from Kraft. "A party from Lalicker's rode onto High Green range early this morning. They killed one man, shot up two others. We're charging Ford Lalicker with murder."

"You're doing what?" Lalicker shouted, his lips working angrily. "You got the gall to say it was my boys that started the shooting?"

"Just what I am doing," Aaron Kraft replied evenly. "Lige Hathaway's dead. Your bunch killed him, trying to get to that bunch of breeding stock I've got corralled in Box Canyon. Was when they stopped them —"

"Bushwhacked — that's what you mean!" Lalicker yelled. "It was your —"

"Hold on!" John Coon cut in loudly. "This ain't going to get nobody no place. Aaron, I was about to ride out, have a talk. Ford says your men started the shooting."

"That's a goddamn lie!"

"Hear me out. He claims his riders were out looking for strays — about a dozen head that'd drifted off his range. Trailed them to your place and was about to catch up when Hathaway and a dozen of your outfit cut loose on them. He says they was lucky to get away with only a couple of them getting wounded."

"Lalicker's a damned liar," Kraft said, his face reddening. "They was trying to get to my breeding stock, either aiming to drive them off or slaughter them, like they've done a lot of my steers."

Starbuck listened in silence. It was strong language — the sort that ordinarily would lead to gun-play — but neither rancher showed any indication of going for his weapon.

"Lige and the boys was waiting for them."

"Waiting?"

"Right. Trevison had been told that Lalicker and some others was going to do some raiding down on my south range — the Meadows. He had a hunch it was a trick to catch us not looking, sucker us off to one end of my land so's there wouldn't be nobody up at the other end where they aimed to do their devilment. He set up a watch at both places. Was dead right, too. Nobody tried anything at the Meadows, showed up instead at

126

Box Canyon — and you was with them, Ford. One of my boys seen —"

"That ain't nothing but a pure lie!" Lalicker declared, swiping at the sweat on his forehead. "Can prove it by Dave Wescott here, and McCroden. We was eating breakfast together this morning."

"That ain't proof of nothing. You'd lie, and they'd swear to it," Kraft shot back. "Anyways, if you wasn't with them, you sent them . . . knew all about it, same as you've been behind all the other trouble I've been having — the burnings and stampedings and shootings . . ."

"You can't prove nothing."

"I've got Lige Hathaway laying dead over at my place waiting to be buried, and six men who traded bullets with your raiding party. They seen who all was there, and they'll swear to it. That's the kind of proof I got."

"Which don't mean a damned thing. I've got a dozen men who'll swear they were jumped by your hired hands while they was out rounding up strays."

John Coon threw up his hands in frustration. "This ain't getting us nowheres! You both claim you got witnesses to what the other'n done, and I can't see no way of telling who's right and who's wrong. Could be you're both right."

"Lige Hathaway's dead, marshal," Starbuck said quietly. "Seems to me that's what you ought to be thinking about."

Lalicker whirled to Shawn. "Now, who the hell are you? You one of them gunslingers Kraft's hired?"

"He is," the rancher snapped. "I done it to protect myself — was you that started it."

"He doing the talking for you?"

"Works for me. I do my own talking, same as always," Kraft said stiffly, and turned to the man he'd said was Dave Wescott. "You still lining up with Lalicker? You still listening to his lies?"

Wescott's shoulders stirred. "Ain't nothing changed, far as I'm concerned."

"That go for you, too?" Kraft continued, putting his glance on McCroden and Mayberry.

Both men nodded. "What you're doing's wrong, Aaron," the latter said. "We just can't let you get away with it."

"Get away with what?"

"With freezing us all out, taking over our places."

Aaron Kraft swore helplessly. "You're blind, plain stone blind — all three of you! I ain't after your damned ranches. Ain't got no use for no more range, and if you had any sense, you could see that Lalicker's flimflamming you. It's just his way of trying to get back at me — drive *me* out."

Coon waved his hands. "Let's don't get sidetracked into that argument again," he said wearily. "Aaron, I sure don't see how you can swear out a murder charge against Ford for Lige Hathaway's killing unless you got somebody that seen him pull the trigger of the gun that done it — and can prove that Lige didn't have a gun and wasn't shooting back."

"Hell, I wasn't even there," Lalicker insisted. "Any man that says I was is a liar. Already told you, John, I can prove where I was."

128

"Maybe you wasn't with them," Kraft admitted, hedging. "Rider of mine only said he thought he seen you, but that don't change the fact that you sent —"

"Two sides to that, too," the lawman broke in. "Way I look at it, there was shooting on both sides. Some of Lalicker's boys got shot, too. Lige was just unlucky enough to get killed."

Aaron Kraft was silent for a long moment. Then: "Reckon this all adds up to you saying you ain't going to do nothing about it."

"What it amounts to. No choice. I don't figure you or Ford either one's got a squawk coming. Your two outfits got in a fight, there was some shooting . . . and you come out on the short end."

Kraft sighed heavily, turned to Trevison. "Guess you were right, son. Going to have to handle things your way."

Boone, slouched against a wall, thumbs hooked on his gunbelt, hat tipped forward over his eyes, smiled. "Only answer — always is."

John Coon bristled. "Just back off there a bit, mister! That sounds like a threat."

Trevison ignored the lawman, nodded to Lalicker. "I give your outfit notice once before that they'd best keep off High Green range. Saying it again, only this time I'm warning you personally — don't you or any of your hired help ever set foot on Mr. Kraft's land again. Goes for you, too, Wescott, and you, McCroden . . . and you, Mayberry. Doing it's the same as signing your own death warrant, because I'll be coming for you."

The sudden tension that had gripped Starbuck eased. He had half-expected Trevison to make a move then and there, bringing the situation to a final, bloody climax. But the gunman appeared satisfied just to repeat his previous threats.

"Same goes for my range," Shawn heard Lalicker say. "I'm speaking for my friends here, too. From now on my crew's got orders to shoot at any High Green rider they catch trespassing."

"They been doing that right along, no matter whose land they was on!" Kraft shouted. "Far as a shooting order goes, I'll be giving the same to my boys — all of them."

Starbuck shook his head. There would never be a meeting of minds insofar as Aaron Kraft and Ford Lalicker were concerned. Stubborn, unreasonable, each would yield not the slightest, but would continue their game of dire promises while they skirted the edge of deadly violence.

"You both better slack off, do a little hard thinking about this," Shawn said, unwilling to give in without at least making an attempt to ease the situation. "There'll be a lot of blood spilled around here if you don't pull in your horns."

"Well, I ain't backing down," Lalicker snapped, and wheeling, moved for the doorway. McCroden and the other two ranchers immediately stepped in behind him, and all passed through the opening out onto the landing. Boone Trevison pivoted smoothly, made as if to follow.

"Be none of that!" John Coon said hurriedly, picking up the pistol lying on his desk. "You just set down there and wait a few minutes. I'll have no shoot-outs on my street."

Trevison scowled, reversed himself, dropped onto one of the chairs. Kraft came about, watched Lalicker and his friends mount up, swing off down the street. Deep lines rutted his face, and the tiredness in his eyes was unmistakable.

"It's the same old story, ain't it, John?" he said without looking at the lawman. "There just ain't nothing you can do about it."

"I keep telling you: when you've got the right kind of proof, I'll do my duty. Lalicker keeps coming to me with the same kind of complaining you do, and I tell him the same thing: get me the proof."

"Lige being dead ain't the kind you want . . ."

"Lige Hathaway being dead only means he run out of luck. It was a shoot-out between your outfit and Lalicker's. He got killed. I'm sorry about that, because Lige was a friend of mine — I liked him, but there ain't nothing to be done on account of it."

"Nothing but bury him, I reckon," Kraft said, a thread of sarcasm riding his tone as he continued to look out into the street. "Your friends've gone. It all right if we leave now?"

Coon's jaw tightened. His eyes glittered briefly, and then, shrugging, he settled down to his desk.

"Suit yourself," he said. "Just don't take the same trail out of town as Lalicker."

CHAPTER
EIGHTEEN

Aaron Kraft seemed pleased as he stepped out into the sunlight and paused. He nodded to Starbuck and to Boone Trevison.

"Just come to me," he said. "Maybe it's all going to end now. There's been a killing — and I'm right sorry about that, so don't go getting no wrong ideas — but I've got a hunch Lige's death jarred Lalicker and them others right down to their boot heels. And it's going to wake up a few folks around here, too, make them see what's going on."

There was a shaft of hope in it, Starbuck agreed. "Probably just as well you didn't push the marshal into arresting somebody for the shooting. That most likely would've started the pot to boiling good again."

"Got you boys to thank for bringing it all to a head."

Trevison smiled broadly. "A man can always figure out how to get a job done if he tries."

Kraft studied the gunman for a few moments, and then, turning, glanced along the street.

"Going to take some fast talking to keep Joe Hathaway from getting back at Lalicker. He's dead set on revenging Lige, and when he finds out we didn't do nothing with the marshal, I expect he'll blow up bigger'n a foundered steer."

"Could be he'll have cooled off by the time we get back," Boone said.

"Maybe. Sure be a shame for him to mess things up, get it all started again now that we've kind of got it leveled off."

Shawn considered the rancher's wishful words. He wasn't so certain anything had ended; to his way of thinking, only a temporary, uneasy truce founded on the death of Lige Hathaway and mutual warnings had been accomplished. And that was but little, if any, improvement over previously existing conditions.

"You know Lalicker and his friends better than I do," Starbuck said. "You think they'll keep their men off your range now?"

"Good chance of it. It's been made plain to them what they can expect if they do any trespassing, and I don't see them, specially Dave Wescott or Mayberry or Eric McCroden, doing anything foolish."

"You didn't mention Lalicker. What about him?"

Kraft scratched at his jaw. "Well, you've met him first-hand, and you can see what kind of a son-of-a-bitch he is. Bullheaded, plain mean, and unreasonable, and with something chawing away at his innards like a beaver gnaws at a pine tree. I kind of think he'll keep his distance, but you just never know about Ford . . . You boys hungry? I could stand a bite of dinner myself. Can go over to Pete Moriarty's."

"Be fine," Trevison said at once. "Me and Shawn got off to an early start this morning and ain't had nothing but coffee since last night."

"Won't take long to fix that," the rancher said, and led the way to the restaurant.

They spent an hour or so over the meal, and when it was finished and they were again on the sidewalk, Kraft halted at its edge.

"Got a little business to talk over with Whistler," he said, jerking a thumb in the direction of the general store. "You can tag along, or I'll meet you at the saloon when I'm done."

"Saloon — the Cattleking — that'll be better," Trevison said. "I ain't much of a hand to stand around waiting while folks are talking business."

Starbuck started to voice his opinion, but Aaron Kraft spoke first. "Fair enough. I'll drop by there when I'm ready to head for home," he said, and moved off for Whistler's.

Boone stepped down into the dust of the street, glanced back at Shawn. The big trail rider hadn't stirred.

"You coming?"

In no need of a drink after his dinner, and suspecting Trevison desired to drop by the Cattleking only in order to savor the after effects of his triumph of the night before, Starbuck continued to hesitate.

He had given some thought to buying himself a new rifle, one of the Winchester lever action models that he'd noticed on display in the window of Austin's gun shop. With extra money in his pocket it would be an opportune time to see if he could strike up a deal with the storekeeper.

But allowing Boone Trevison to go into the saloon alone could be asking for trouble. The gunman had given him the impression several times since they'd gone to work for Aaron Kraft that he was only too willing to draw and use the worn forty-five pistol hanging on his hip. And with the situation along the Packsaddles as precarious as it was at that moment, it might not be wise to let him visit the saloon alone.

There could be friends of Lalicker, or of one of the ranchers who sided him, that might make a remark at which Trevison would take offense; and a shooting now, during what Kraft felt was an easing of tension and the possibility of peace settling over the country, would certainly bring it all to a quick halt.

"Yeh, reckon so," Starbuck said grudgingly, and left the walk. He could see about the rifle later. Best he do all he could to keep things from blowing sky-high, if indeed there had been a chance.

His concern was for nothing. There were only two patrons in the Cattleking at that hour, and both seemed unaware of who Boone Trevison might be. The bartender was polite but remote when he greeted them at the counter, and served them without comment. Taking up his glass, Shawn moved to one of the tables in the half-dark room and sat down. Trevison, failing to get anything more than monosyllabic answers when he attempted to draw the barman into a conversation, soon joined him.

135

"Figured there'd be more of a crowd here," the gunman complained, pulling out a chair and settling onto it. His keen disappointment was evident. "Asked the barkeep where everybody was. Said it was too early. Makes no sense to me — hell, a drink goes good anytime of the day."

Boone could be expected to look at it that way, Shawn supposed. A man in his profession, who ordinarily had nothing but time on his hands, would find it difficult to understand why others — excluding the barflies and confirmed drunks, of course — with obligations to employers or to their own businesses, would necessarily restrict their attendance in a saloon to afterhours.

"All depends on how you make a living," Shawn said.

Trevison yawned, stretched, downed his liquor. Out in the street, the quick drum of horses hurrying by set up a hollow beat inside the nearly deserted building. Boone beckoned to the bartender, motioning for him to bring the bottle of whiskey and refill his glass. The solemn-faced man complied, turned away when Starbuck shook his head.

"You ain't much of a drinker," Boone observed slyly. "You got something against liquor?"

"No. I've drunk my share — just don't feel the need for it right now."

Trevison took a swallow from his glass, looked around the empty room. "Place could sure use some customers. I've been in graveyards that was livelier than this."

136

"Be different at night," Shawn said, and felt a flow of relief as Aaron Kraft came through the doorway, paused, and advanced toward them.

"You want a drink?" the gunman asked as the rancher halted at their table.

"Don't mind if I do," Kraft said, dropping back to the bar. He waited while the man behind the counter filled a glass, and then, bringing it to the table, sat down.

"Everything all right around here?" he asked.

"Fine. Fine. Place's dead, but Shawn here figures that's how it ought to be. Where I come from, a man can find a saloon going strong day and night."

"Expect so," Kraft said laconically, and tossing off his whiskey, got to his feet. "I'm ready to head back if you all are."

"Anytime," Starbuck said, rising.

Trevison drained his glass, drew himself erect. The liquor seemed to have hit him hard. His eyes were unusually bright, and he was slightly unsteady. For a man who drank considerable, it was something of a puzzle to Shawn, but he said nothing.

Returning to the street, they doubled back to the hitchrack fronting the jail, where their horses were picketed, and mounting up under the steady, noncommittal stare of John Coon, rode out of the settlement and onto the road that would take them to High Green.

The ride was made in silence, and a time later, after they had dropped off the hogback and were swinging toward the yard, Aaron Kraft drew up worriedly on his saddle.

"What do you reckon's going on down there?" he wondered, pointing to the bunkhouse.

Starbuck's attention also was on the dozen or so men gathered in front of the crew's quarters. "Looks like something's happened," he replied, and raked his horse with his spurs.

They came onto the hardpack at a gallop, slowed as Leda appeared on the porch of the main house and hurried to meet them. Her face was taut, strained.

"What's the matter, girl?" the rancher asked, leaving the saddle. "Something gone wrong?"

"Couldn't be much worse," she answered. "Joe Hathaway's killed Ford Lalicker."

CHAPTER
NINETEEN

"God in heaven!" Aaron Kraft breathed. "That sure puts the fat in the fire now."

"What can we do?" Leda said anxiously. "There's a bunch from Lalicker's, and from some of the other ranches, too, coming after Joe."

"Lynch party," Starbuck muttered, and wheeling, crossed the yard to the bunkhouse.

Hathaway was in the center of the riders. He had collected his gear, was hurriedly loading it onto his horse preparatory to flight. He looked up as Shawn, off his sorrel now and followed by Kraft, Leda, and Boone Trevison, broke into the circle of men.

"I ain't sorry I done it," he said belligerently.

Kraft shook his head angrily. "Was a damn fool stunt, Joe, and you know it. Why'd you change your mind? When I left here this morning you told us you'd wait till we got back from town before you did something."

The young cowhand stirred. "Just kept thinking about Lige and how it wasn't right for him to be laying there dead while the man that got him killed was strutting around alive — big as you please. Got a couple of the boys to give me a hand and buried him, then we rode over to Lalicker's, and I called him out."

"Who was with you?" Starbuck asked. The men accompanying Joe Hathaway would be equally objects of the lynch mob.

"Was Hugh Dixon, there, and Earl White — but don't go blaming them, or worrying about them, either. I made them wait back in the piñon grove south of the place, out of sight, while I took care of Lalicker."

"He by himself?" Trevison asked.

"Yeh. I just rode up to the door, yelled for him. When he come out, I emptied my gun into him and left. Heard a lot of hollering when I did, and I seen a couple of jaspers come running around the side of the house, but they was too late to do any shooting . . . I got to get riding, Mr. Kraft. Sure be obliged to you if I could draw what wages I got coming. Don't want to be around here anywheres when that bunch shows up."

"There'll be trouble whether you're here or not," Starbuck said bluntly. "Can figure on Lalicker's crew getting back at High Green right along with making you pay for shooting him."

"Done what I had to do," Hathaway said doggedly, buckling his saddlebags. "Knew you'd not get the marshal to help any . . . You didn't, did you?"

Kraft said, "Had a talk with Ford Lalicker and the others. Happened they was in Coon's office when we got there. Thrashed things out good, and I figure we come to a sort of understanding. Chances are everything'd a cooled down plenty, but now, after this stunt you've pulled —"

140

"Maybe so," Hathaway cut in, "but you ain't never answered my question yet. Was the marshal going to do something about Lige's killing?"

Kraft looked down. "No, said there wasn't nothing he could do in a case like this. Was a shoot-out, and Lige was unlucky."

"Just what I figured," Hathaway said, nodding. "Man has to do his own snake-skinning. My pa always said that, and this sure proves it . . . Can I draw my wages, Mr. Kraft?"

The rancher's shoulders lifted, fell. "Sure. Got some cash up at the house. I'll have to go get it."

"Be obliged to you. Time's kind of short for me . . ."

"It's already too late, Joe," Starbuck said as Aaron Kraft wheeled, started across the yard. "I don't know what you're aiming to do, but running won't work. They'll catch you sooner or later — if not here in the Packsaddle country, some other place."

"Ain't got no choice."

"Sure you have," Boone Trevison said firmly. "Can stay right here and fight. There's enough of us to stand up to that Lalicker outfit, give them a hell of a lot more'n they're bargaining for."

"Only get some people killed," Shawn said. "My advice is to go into town, turn yourself over to the marshal."

"The law'll only string him up, same as that lynch mob's fixing to do," Harmon protested.

Starbuck glanced around. Most of the men present, while employees of High Green, were strangers to him;

the only ones he knew besides Harmon were Hugh Dixon, Tom Orr, and Dan Chesser.

"He'll hang for sure if he runs and gets caught. Turning himself in and offering to go before a judge will be in his favor. Good chance he'll get off with a term in the territorial pen."

"That wouldn't be much better'n hanging," Hathaway said glumly.

"Living always beats dying," Starbuck countered. "My guess is, when the judge hears your story, he'll go easy on you."

"Lalicker was a big rancher. Judge'll be for him," Hathaway continued, and glanced to Kraft's daughter. "What do you think Miss Leda?"

"I think you ought to listen to Starbuck," the girl said. "And far as Ford Lalicker having influence, my father is a big man around here, too, and he can do you a lot of good."

The sound of Kraft's returning at a run brought a stop to the conversation. Face flushed from the exertion, the rancher drew up before Hathaway. Extending his arm, he dropped several gold coins into the puncher's hand.

"What you've got coming . . . and a little extra."

Joe looked down at the money, his weathered brow pulled into tight lines. The rancher studied him wonderingly.

"What's the matter — ain't it enough?"

"No, not that. More here than I got coming, but we've been talking, and Starbuck figures the best thing I can do is turn myself in to the marshal for a trial. Says

142

I ain't got a chance — even if I give that Lalicker bunch the slip."

"He's right," Kraft said promptly. "Be the smartest thing you can do."

"Was I to listen to him, would you stand up for me in court, tell the judge how things was?"

"Can bank on it, Joe. And I'll get you a lawyer, too — a good one that'll look out for you."

Hathaway glanced about at the men forming a loose half-circle around him. He seemed to be seeking confirmation, some assurance that it was the right thing to do from them. No comments were forthcoming.

Shawn turned his attention to the north. "When'd you leave Lalicker's?"

"About noon."

Evidently the rancher had met his death not long after he'd ridden out of Carsonville and reached home. That would now be three or four hours ago.

"Better get your deciding done," he said gently. "That lynch mob's about had time to get here."

"You know for sure one's coming?" Kraft asked.

"Ain't no doubt," Hugh Dixon said. "I sort of hung around after Joe rode out. Could hear them yelling, getting together. Charlie Vine was heading up things, hollering orders like he was a general or something. Sent a couple of men off to bring in the riders that was working cattle on the range, another'n over to Wescott's place. Aims to show up with a regular army, I reckon." Dixon paused, shook his head warningly at Hathaway. "Like Starbuck there says, Joe, you'd better make up your mind pretty quick. They'll be showing up before long."

Hathaway's shoulders slumped. "Expect I'll just turn myself in," he said. "Ain't no hand at running and hiding, and if Mr. Kraft and Starbuck both figures it's the right thing to do, then I guess it is. Sure be obliged if a couple of you'll ride in with me."

"We'll all go," Shawn said, turning to Dixon and the others. "Get your horses. We ride out in five minutes."

It wasn't necessary to tell the riders to come armed; all were wearing weapons and had been, he supposed, since trouble came to the Packsaddle country.

"Glad you thought of that," Kraft said, dropping a hand on Shawn's shoulder as they turned to mount up. "Just might run into that bunch."

"What I'm afraid of. Little surprised they haven't got here already," Starbuck said, and frowning, nodded toward Leda, climbing the steps to the porch at the rear of the house. "Wonder now if we ought to leave a few men here to look after your daughter . . . and the place."

"I can stay," Trevison volunteered at once.

Kraft glanced about. "No, could be you'll be bad needed on the road if that lynch mob cuts in ahead of us on the way to town . . . Don't like leaving my girl alone, however."

"Probably best you stay," Starbuck said. "And we can spare a couple of men. Chances are about even we won't run into that bunch."

"Well, if you do, you won't have enough guns as it is. But you've got a good idea — I wouldn't be no good to you anyway. I'll hang around here. Can get the cook, and there's probably a couple of yard hands and a wrangler or two around back.

"May even be a couple of the boys asleep in the bunkhouse. I'll roust them out and fort up here in the house. You head on into town with Joe and see that Coon locks him up safe — then hustle right on back. Might be needing you."

Starbuck indicated his agreement and swung onto the sorrel. He waited while Trevison went onto his horse and then rode back to the center of the hardpack, where Joe Hathaway and the men who would be forming the escort were gathered.

"Want you in the center, Joe," he said, and motioned for the others to close in around him.

"Ain't aiming to let nobody take a potshot at me, that it?" the puncher said with a wry grin.

"I'm expecting to get you to town alive," Starbuck replied, seeing no humor in the situation, and let his eyes run over the riders, mentally ticking them off, counting, recalling names.

Earlier there had been nine men, including Hathaway — an even dozen when he, Kraft, and Boone Trevison added their presence to the group. Now there were only ten; with the rancher gone, there should be eleven in the party. Slowing, he studied the riders as they moved out of the yard and pointed for the distant hogback.

In that next moment it came to him; Dan Chesser was missing.

CHAPTER
TWENTY

Starbuck spurred up alongside Hugh Dixon. As the man turned to him, he said, "Where'd Dan Chesser go?"

Dixon, puzzled, glanced about. "Hell, I didn't know he'd gone! Seen him heading for his horse. Never paid no more attention to him after that."

Shawn swung away, eased in beside Trevison. "Chesser's pulled out on us."

"Pulled out?" the gunman echoed blankly. "Why?"

"Probably to join up with that bunch coming for Hathaway. Proves what I've been thinking: he's the one that's been double-crossing Kraft — the one that tried bushwhacking us."

"That means they'll know for sure we're taking Joe Hathaway to town, and will be figuring to cut us off."

"Can bet on it. I've got a plan that'll maybe fool them. You get up in front, keep your eyes peeled."

Trevison started to make some reply, but Starbuck, fearing time was an all-important factor, wheeled away, and shouldering his horse through those of the other riders, drew in beside Hathaway.

Motioning to Dixon, he said, "Joe, I want you to swap your hat and jacket with Hugh. Horse, too."

Both men stared at him. "Good chance that lynch mob knows we're heading into town — thanks to Dan Chesser."

"Chesser?" Hathaway said, surprised. "You saying he's working for Lalicker?"

"Pretty sure of it — and we won't gamble on me being wrong. What I want is for you and Hugh to change places."

Dixon nodded. "Then, if they move in on us, Joe can slip off for town on his own, because they'll be watching me — thinking I'm him."

"That's it. Like as not we'll be outnumbered plenty, and this is one way maybe Joe can make it to the marshal's office."

At once Dixon and Hathaway began to make the exchange, doing so without bringing the party, now nearing the crest of the hogback, to a halt. Shawn waited until it was complete, and then, moving Hathaway, looking very much like Dixon from even a short distance, to a rear, flanking position in the party, resumed his place in the front. Trevison, his face solemn, greeted him with a nod.

"This here plan of yours —"

"All set. Got Dixon to trade places with Joe. If we get stopped, Hathaway'll slip off and line out for town by himself. It'll work, long as they mistake Dixon for him."

"You figure that'll fool them?"

"Ought to. You see any signs of riders down the way?"

"Nope — nothing. Maybe it was all talk."

"Doubt that. They've hardly had time to cut across and stop us along here. My guess is they'll be waiting somewhere along the foot of the mountain. Chesser could have met them, told them what was up. All they'd had to do then was ride straight across the slope from Lalicker's."

Trevison shifted on his saddle. "You got a plan for us too — for when they jump us?"

Starbuck reined in the sorrel, steadying the big horse as he clattered across the stone surface of the hogback's summit.

"Only thing we can do is talk," he said. "Try to make them see reason. If that doesn't work, it'll come down to your way of settling arguments — gunplay."

Trevison looked over his shoulder, let his gaze sweep the riders tightly grouped behind him. "Odds'll be mighty bad if we try that. They're only a bunch of cowhands."

"Never figured you for one who'd worry about the odds."

Boone shrugged. "I don't. Only, there ain't no sense in being plumb foolish at a time like this. Might be better was we to make a run for it instead of trying to talk."

Surprise rolled through Starbuck. He considered the gunman in silence for a long minute. He'd never expected to hear a statement such as that come from him, and it stirred into life a thread of doubt in his mind, gave rise to the question: *Am I doing this right?*

The fact that an experienced gunfighter, a hired killer like Boone Trevison, would suggest they turn and run was disturbing. Could he be leading nine men and himself to their deaths? But running would be no solution; they would only turn the situation into a gun battle on horseback.

"We'd been better off to've stayed there at the ranch, fort up, like Aaron's doing," Trevison went on. "Could've scattered ourselves around the place, laid low, and when that bunch rode in, let them have it."

"Be one way of doing it, all right," Starbuck agreed. "Would've meant a lot of men getting killed, maybe even the Krafts getting hurt, besides the damage that would have been done. You can be sure they would set fire to everything they could get to — bunch like that gets out of hand quick. They'd not stop until the place was in ashes and all the people trying to hold them off had quit . . . or were dead. Talking to them like I aim to just maybe'll avoid all that."

"Be a plenty of them dead too — same as there'll likely be with us trying it your way."

"Not saying you're wrong, but way I see it, it'll probably boil down to just you and me against Vine and those two that hang around with him — Rearick and Bill Bristol."

Trevison straightened on his saddle. "How you going to manage that?"

"Not saying I can. Aim to try and talk them all into backing off, letting the law take its course. Pretty sure most of them will cool off and listen, but I'm just as sure Charlie Vine and his sidekicks won't. That'll put it flat up to you and me."

Boone made no comment, and Shawn put his attention to the road winding down the mountainside ahead of them. They were moving through the heavily forested area of thickly growing tall pines and dense clumps of oak, with mahogany and other shrubs crowding in close. They were near halfway down the slope, Starbuck reckoned, and if he had judged correctly, they would soon encounter the Lalicker party.

Who would be in the lynch mob? That Vine, Rearick, and Bristol would be at the head was a foregone conclusion, and there would be those who worked for Lalicker and believed it their duty to take part in avenging his death. McCroden, Wescott, and Mayberry — they were the ones in question. Would they be there?

It would help the situation if they were. All appeared to be reasonable men more or less caught up in a fight they would as soon have no part of. He should be able to talk to them, make them understand that Joe Hathaway was the law's business, and that a lynching would only make matters worse for everybody.

But he could not expect Charlie Vine and his two partners — and possibly a couple other diehard Lalicker cowhands — to settle for such. They were of the same stripe as Boone Trevison — men who believed that a gun was the only answer.

Trevison, however, was making sounds like his ideas along those lines were changing somewhat. Just why, it was hard to understand — unless it was Leda Kraft who had brought it about. She'd made it clear at the outset that her opinion of gunfighters was very low.

150

Boone had taken note of that, and since his interest in Aaron Kraft's daughter was apparent from the start, he could be attempting to change his ways. That Leda's estimation of him had altered considerably since his arrival at High Green was evidenced by her subsequent accepting him as she had — treating him to coffee and dessert at the house and holding lengthy conversations whenever the opportunity arose, which hadn't been often, to be sure, but they both had made the best of it. Just how far it —

"Something moving down the way a piece."

At the low warning from one of the riders, Starbuck threw his glance to a bend in the road a short quarter-mile on below. He caught a fleeting glimpse of a horse moving through the brush.

"That'll be them," he said in a tight voice, and turned to Hathaway, riding at the edge of the party on its opposite side. "Joe, when we come to that next stand of brush growing close to the road, turn off and get out of sight. Stay put until you see us stop, then circle wide and light out for town . . . You haven't changed your mind about handing yourself over to the marshal, have you?"

"Sure ain't," Hathaway replied.

"All right . . . Good luck."

"Obliged — and same to you, and to all you boys."

Shawn came back to the remaining riders. "I'm hoping this won't get no farther than talk, and I'm going to try and keep them at that long as I can, so's Joe'll have plenty of time to get away. Just forget you're

151

packing a gun. If it comes to shooting, I'll say when. Everybody understand?"

There was a murmur of assurance. Starbuck shifted to Hugh Dixon. "Keep your head down, so's they won't see your face. Longer we keep them thinking you're Joe, the better off we'll be."

"I'll sort of stay in front of him," Tom Orr suggested. "That'll make it hard for them to get a good look."

Starbuck nodded. He could feel the increase of tension among the men, and as they drew abreast of the dense clump of juniper and oak extending out onto the shoulder of the road and Joe Hathaway drifted off and out of sight, a complete silence fell over them. Each was wondering, probably, what the next few minutes held for him and if he'd be alive to see that day's sunset.

"There they are . . ."

Trevison's voice was taut, carried a note of uncertainty — or perhaps it was the tight, steellike anticipation that grips all men at such critical moments.

"Keep remembering," Starbuck cautioned softly, "no shooting unless I give the word," and concentrated on the riders spreading out to block the road ahead.

CHAPTER
TWENTY-ONE

"Far as you're going!"

It was Charlie Vine. Starbuck raised his hand, brought the men behind him to a halt. He raked Lalicker's gunman with a glance, let his eyes drift on to the others in the lynching party. Bill Bristol and Al Rearick were at each of Vine's shoulders, Chesser was close by, and strung out to either side were Ford Lalicker's riders. Shawn breathed a bit easier; the group included ranchers Dave Wescott and Eric McCroden.

"What's this all about?" he demanded, knowing well the answer but beginning his play for time.

"Don't be giving us that hogwash!" Vine snarled, reaching for a coil of rope hanging from his saddlehorn and brandishing it overhead. "We're wanting Joe Hathaway there, and we aim to get him!"

"Not till we've done some talking," Starbuck replied coldly. He faced the two ranchers. "You realize what you're making yourself a part of?"

McCroden glanced at Wescott, bobbed. "You're goddamn right we do! We're stringing up the jasper that killed Ford."

"That's the law's job," Shawn said. "I'm telling you all to turn around and go home. It's all over nothing, anyway."

"Over nothing!" Vine shouted. "Kraft's been leading up to this for months — out trying to grab onto the whole damned country and —"

"That's a lie, Charlie. Maybe you don't know that, but it is. Kraft's not after anybody's land — he's got more now than he needs. Wescott, you ever hear it from anybody but Lalicker that he was out to get your ranch? You either, McCroden?"

Again the ranchers exchanged looks. Wescott stirred uneasily. "Well, no, can't say as I have."

"Nobody else can, either. Was Ford Lalicker put that idea in your minds. He's had it in for Kraft . . . has for years, in fact, ever since Aaron beat him to filing on High Green. Wanted it himself."

"Hell, that was twenty, thirty years ago," one of Lalicker's men said. "You telling us it's been festering inside him all this time?"

"Just what I'm saying. Expect the answer is that Lalicker was too busy building up his own place all those years in between to think about it. Then, when he got things to where he didn't have anything to do but coast along, he started stewing about how he came in second best to Kraft and decided to do something about it."

Charlie Vine spat. "That don't have nothing to do with Joe Hathaway murdering him."

"Has everything to do with it. It's the reason behind it. Lige Hathaway would be alive right now if Ford

Lalicker hadn't made up his mind to start trouble with Kraft."

"Jace," McCroden said after a short silence, "you been around Ford ever since he got his place going. It true what Starbuck there said — that Ford wanted High Green but Aaron Kraft beat him to it?"

An elderly cowhand sitting his horse quietly nearby the rancher nodded slowly. "Reckon that's the how of it. Kraft just got there ahead of Ford."

"And there wasn't nothing crooked about it?"

Jace wagged his head. "Nothing. Ford seen the country, figured it was where he wanted to start his ranch. Went to file on it, make all them paper arrangements, whatever they are, but they told him at the land office it'd already been took by a fellow named Kraft. Know that's how it was, 'cause I was there with him."

"He drop it then, or did he try to get it anyway?"

"Well, weren't nothing he could do about it, but he did go see Aaron, offered to buy him out, but Aaron weren't interested in selling. Ford then took some land on to the north. Was just as good as High Green, far as I could see, but Ford always did hate not getting what he first wanted."

Again there was a silence, broken only by the restless shifting of the horses and the distant moaning of a dove.

"This trouble Lalicker claims Kraft caused — there anything to that?"

Jace looked down. His slight shoulders stirred. "Don't know nothing about that — my job's punching cows, and I kept my nose out of other goings-on."

155

"But you knew about it," Wescott pressed, following up McCroden's question. "I know that some of Kraft's boys raided Lalicker's herds a couple of times."

"Yeh, they sure did!"

"Who started the raiding — that's what we're trying to get at."

The old cowhand wiped away the sweat on his seamed, weathered face. Shawn glanced at the riders. All were watching the man intently, awaiting his reply — all except Charlie Vine, who was flipping the rope he held back and forth in angry impatience.

"We can use the truth here, Jace," Starbuck said. "Whatever you say won't help or hurt Ford Lalicker, but it could keep some of your friends from dying."

Jace considered Shawn's words, his grizzled features a blank. Then: "Yeh, reckon you're right, mister. It was Ford that started it. Was like you already said — not getting High Green just kept biting at him until it finally busted loose and made him take it into his head to do something about it . . . Shame, too. Ford was a mighty fine fellow once. He just let his wantings get the best of him."

"Which still don't mean nothing now!" Vine declared loudly. "He was murdered right on his own doorstep, and me for one aims to see the man that done it swing!"

"He will, if the law says so," Starbuck said, flicking a look at Trevison. The talking was about over. He'd made his point, and the lynch mob would either back off now and leave — or there would be shooting.

156

"Hathaway's already gone into town. He's turning himself over to the marshal."

"The hell! I can see him setting right there behind Tom Orr," Vine declared.

"That ain't Joe!" Dan Chesser came back in a surprised voice. "That there's Dixon. He's wearing Joe's hat and coat, and riding his horse."

Vine swore, said something aside to Rearick and Bristol. Eric McCroden rose in his stirrups, looked about at the men strung around him.

"I'm for calling this off. Ain't no doubt in my mind now that Lalicker bamboozled the lot of us — was just using us to buck Aaron Kraft."

"Goddamnit!" Vine shouted. "We ain't doing no such a thing! It still don't make no difference far as the killing goes. Man that done that —"

"Man that done that's handed himself over to John Coon," McCroden cut in coldly. "Ends that part of it, too."

Dave Wescott nodded his confirmation of McCroden's words. "Let's just move on, forget what we was aiming to do . . . Too late, anyway. Joe Hathaway ain't here."

"Ain't never too late," Vine said. "Be no big chore riding into town and busting him out of that crackerbox jail — and that old man wearing a tin star ain't going to give us no trouble."

"Forget it," Starbuck warned tautly. "Let it stop here without any more blood being spilled."

"Hell with that!"

"Then you're going to have to ride through Trevison and me — and maybe a couple more men."

"Can tell you this, Charlie," McCroden said bluntly. "If you try it, it won't be with me helping."

"Same goes for me," Wescott said, and faced the riders. "Take my advice, pull out, go on back to the ranch. What Vine's talking is plain foolish."

Several of the men stirred, began to move away. Vine wheeled on them furiously.

"Hold it! We're going right on with what we figured to do — string up the bastard that murdered the boss! If Wescott and McCroden want to coyote out on us, let them. We don't need them — we got more'n enough to get the job done."

Starbuck, nerves steeling for what he knew was inevitable, cast a side look at Boone Trevison. The gunman was rigid on his saddle, both hands resting on the horn. His eyes were filled with a wildness, and the skin of his face was stretched tight across the bones.

"We're standing by you, Starbuck," Hugh Dixon murmured. "Just you say the word."

Shawn shook his head. "Trouble between High Green and Lalicker is over and done with. There'll be no shooting — no killing. It's come down to a personal matter. Trevison and me against Vine and his two friends."

"Who says?" Charlie demanded, frowning.

"I do . . . And if you don't believe it, look behind you."

Vine threw a glance over his shoulder. Not only had McCroden and Dave Wescott pulled back out of the way, but Lalicker's crew as well. Even Chesser had declared himself by drawing off to the side.

158

Vine shrugged, grinned tightly. "Don't make no difference to me . . . I reckon me and Bill and Al will be enough. What about them jaspers behind you? They in or out?"

"Out," Shawn said quietly, and not taking his eyes off Charlie, waved the men from Kraft's off the road. When the muffled sound of the horses in motion had ceased, he nodded to Lalicker's gunmen.

"Up to you now. Either forget Joe Hathaway . . . or make your move."

Vine chose the latter course. Starbuck saw the slight break in the man's expression, threw himself to one side. Drawing fast, he fired. Vine jolted, rocked back, began to fall from his saddle. In that same fragment of time Starbuck felt the solid, searing wallop of a bullet from either Rearick's or Bristol's gun slam into his leg. He triggered again, his target Rearick. Fired a third time, at Bristol. Both men buckled, began to slide from their horses, now shying nervously in the drifting layers of pungent powder smoke.

Taut, pistol still leveled and ready, Starbuck rode out the tension-filled moments, his narrow glance fastened to the three men, while the fire in his leg built steadily to flaming proportions. And then slowly he relaxed. Vine was on the ground, face in the dust; Rearick and Bill Bristol were sprawled nearby, unmoving Vaguely he heard someone in the silently watching party of Lalicker men speak in an awed, breathless way.

"My God . . ."

His shoulders went down at that. He turned to Trevison. Boone was frozen on his saddle, hands still locked to the horn. A look of abject fear covered his sweaty face. He had not stirred. A deep anger swept through Shawn.

"I don't know who the hell you are," he grated in a low, savage voice, "but you're not Boone Trevison!"

CHAPTER
TWENTY-TWO

Starbuck, jaw set against the pain raging in his leg, rocked back slightly, holstered his pistol. Riders were crowding up — both High Green and Lalicker — having their look at him, making their awkward congratulations. Several had dismounted, were bending over the lifeless bodies of Charlie Vine and his two friends.

"You bad hit?"

It was Eric McCroden. Beside him was Wescott. Both ranchers, off their horses, were standing at his knee.

Shawn shrugged. "Bleeding some. I've been hurt worse."

Wescott pulled a folded red bandanna from a pocket. "Here . . . let me have a look at it," he said. "Can use this for a bandage until you see Doc Eiseman. It's clean."

Starbuck only nodded, sat quietly on his horse while the rancher cut a slit in his pants leg, uncovering the wound, and then wrapped the cloth about it.

"That'll slow down the bleeding. Looks like only a flesh wound . . . but you best get to Eiseman soon as you can."

"Aim to," Starbuck said. "You take care of them?" he added, pointing to Vine and the others.

"Sure," McCroden replied, and turning, called to the Lalicker men to load up the bodies of the gunmen on their horses and head back to the ranch.

The hard core of tightness had drained from Starbuck entirely, and he watched the riders go about the grim task of picking up the dead men, drape them across their saddles, and secure them so they would not slide off during the return trip. He sighed heavily.

"It shouldn't have come down to this. Was hoping all along that —"

"Vine was a bad one," Dave Wescott cut in, "so don't go blaming yourself for anything. He would've never let it go, never been satisfied until he'd killed somebody or got himself killed. Come right down to it, I don't think Ford Lalicker was bargaining for the likes of Charlie and them two with him, and maybe — just maybe — this thing with Kraft would've cooled off if Vine hadn't been around to keep prodding him."

"Well, it's over now," McCroden said. "I figure we owe you some thanks, Starbuck — thanks you earned the hard way."

Shawn stirred, looked up. Lalicker's riders were moving off, striking for the ranch. He twisted slowly, gently about, faced the High Green crew. They were waiting quietly for word from him as to what should be done next. He gave them a worn grin.

"Might as well get back to work," he said. "I'll appreciate your telling Aaron Kraft what happened, and that everything's settled."

"And we'll be obliged to you if you'll tell him we'll see him in church Sunday," McCroden added, mounting his horse.

Hugh Dixon, evident spokesman for the crew, bobbed, said, "Sure enough," to the rancher, and then, frowning, faced Shawn. "Where you going if you ain't coming with us?"

"Into town, get my leg fixed up," Starbuck answered, and glanced at Trevison, silent and unmoving during the moments succeeding the shoot-out. "Boone'll ride in with me . . . Look for us about dark."

Dixon said, "Sure enough," again, and wheeling about, put the High Green riders into motion with a wave of his hand.

Starbuck watched them briefly, came back around, and settled his attention on Trevison. His features were hard-set, his voice low and unyielding when he spoke.

"Before we move out for town, I want to know who you are."

The man calling himself Boone Trevison sighed heavily. "Name's Duckworth — Henry Duckworth. I ain't nobody."

Starbuck swung his sorrel onto the road. Understanding was dawning swiftly — explanations as to the man's strange actions and untypical words. "Start talking. Like to know what this is all about — you damn near got me killed."

Duckworth stirred wearily. "Going to be a mite hard to explain, make you see . . ."

"Try me," Shawn said coldly.

Again the man shifted. "Reckon I sure looked like a fool in front of all those men. Worse, I expect — an out-and-out coward, and that's what I guess I am, because I was plain scared clean down to the bone. Couldn't move a finger to help you, even when I knew there was a chance you'd die . . . Don't see how I can ever face up to any of those people again."

"You can if you've got a strong enough reason. They'll think a hell of a lot more of you if you come out and admit you fooled them, and let them know you're sorry for doing it. Wrong to just let it ride."

"Expect you're right, but doing it, looking the Krafts in the eye — especially Leda . . ."

"Same goes double for them — but you haven't got around to answering all I want to know. What made you think you could pass yourself off for a gunslinger like Boone Trevison?"

"Didn't know that's what he was."

Starbuck frowned. "Then how . . . ?"

"Started down in Texas," Duckworth said, pulling off his hat and running fingers nervously through his hair. "I was working on a little hard-scrabble farm — handyman, nothing else mostly. One day I was looking for some stray hogs, fellow had about a dozen, and I came across a dead man laying in the brush.

"He'd been shot in the chest. Guess he was trying to reach someplace where he could get some help, but didn't make it. I went through his pockets aiming to find out who he was, when I come across this letter from Aaron Kraft offering him a job."

"And you decided to become Boone Trevison and take it."

Duckworth nodded. "I figured it was just a regular job punching cows, or maybe even being a foreman, which I figured I could do if somebody'd only give me the chance. I went back to the shed at the farm where I was working, got a spade, and after changing clothes with the dead man — everything but his shirt, because it was all covered with blood — I buried him. Then I got on his horse, which was standing off to the side, and rode out. Told one of the neighbors I run into a bit later to tell the fellow I was working for that I'd quit.

"You pretty well know the story from there on. I headed north for Kraft's. Had to ask my way a few times; then I run into you. I never did know that Boone Trevison was a hired gun until we talked to Kraft."

Starbuck leaned to one side, easing the throbbing pain in his leg by putting his weight on the other. "Lucky you didn't come up against somebody that knew Trevison."

"Realize that, and I guess I was gambling some. But I figured it was worth it. Hell, I'm a man who never had nothing, never amounted to nothing — and I never would, either, way things kept going for me. Turning into Boone Trevison, a man that was dead, looked like a good chance to become somebody and find a decent life."

"Which puts you back where you were at the start, only with different problems," Shawn said flatly. "Both the Krafts like you — how you going to explain all this to them?"

165

"That's what's bothering me most. Expect I could rustle up enough guts to face the crew and tell them what a liar and a fool I was. But Leda — I ain't so sure. Girl means a lot to me, and I was hoping I'd start meaning something to her, but I reckon this'll about close that door for me . . . About all I can figure to do is keep on riding."

"Maybe not," Starbuck said, again shifting. The pain in his leg was mounting steadily as the anesthesia continued to wear off. "I remember she didn't think much of gunmen. Finding out you aren't one ought to be in your favor."

"I don't know," Duckworth said doubtfully. "Lying to her, and acting big when I ain't nothing but a twobit four-flusher . . ."

"You tell her that, see how she takes it."

"Probably won't even listen."

"Give her a chance. There's nothing like the pure truth to get things squared away. She might flare up at first because you fooled her, but that could pass — 'specially if you mean something to her."

"Not sure, but I kind of think I do. Same goes for her pa. I believe he'd like to have me around as his son-in-law. He's getting old, and he's looking for somebody to take over the ranch, run it for him. Was talking along that line the night I was up at the house."

"What you need to do, then, is go back, set them both down, and lay it all out on the table for them. Folks are a lot more forgiving than most people think. And when you get down to the bottom of it, you didn't hurt anybody, you did some good."

166

"Almost got you killed, said so yourself . . ."

"No denying that," Starbuck said wryly. "But I understand why now, and I can forget it. I'm pretty sure the Krafts can overlook the lie you played on them, too."

Duckworth sighed again, this time in relief. "I sure feel better," he said. "Maybe there is some hope for me . . . When you get your leg doctored up, you mind going back to the ranch with me and helping me talk it out with them?"

"I'll be going back, but it'll be to get my gear," Shawn said. "Straightening things out with the Krafts is something you'll have to do on your own. I can't help you there."

Duckworth was quiet for a long minute, seemingly listening to the barking of a dog off in the distance. Then: "Yeh, I've leaned on you enough. Time I stood on my own two feet and took what I got coming, whatever it is . . . You said you was getting your gear — that mean you're moving on?"

Starbuck nodded. "I'm looking for my brother. If the doc can fix me up so's I can ride, I'll head out. I won't find him here."

Henry Duckworth smiled. "You can say you found me — the real me. I'm obliged to you for that."

"Not sure the pleasure was all mine," Shawn said dryly, looking ahead. Carsonville was now in sight. "But you're welcome, just the same."